"It wouldn't need to be a real marriage. It can just be a piece of paper between us. All I need is someone for the baby."

Jake made his words even clearer. "You'll be able to get it annulled in the spring if you want."

He'd do whatever she wanted in that regard.

Elizabeth stood there looking sad. "I just buried my husband. I don't need another one."

"I can make you a marker for that grave if you agree to help me. We can get a good-sized piece of granite sent down from Fort Benton. It'll last forever."

Elizabeth was looking at him now.

"I could carve your daughter's name on it for you."

Elizabeth just stood there, blinking.

"Don't cry," Jake said.

"I never cry," Elizabeth whispered and then took a deep breath. "You have yourself a deal."

Now it was Jake's turn to be surprised into silence. Being married, even temporarily, to a woman with eyes like that couldn't be all bad. He'd just have to think of ways to keep her happy until she decided to leav

D0958435

JANET TRONSTAD

grew up on a small farm in central Montana. One of her favorite things to do was to visit her grandfather's bookshelves, where he had a large collection of Zane Grey novels. She's always loved a good story. Today Janet lives in Pasadena, California, where she is a full-time writer.

Calico Christmas at Dry Creek

JANET TRONSTAD

Steeple
Hill®

Published by Steeple Hill Books™

STEEPLE HILL BOOKS

Steeple
Hill®

ISBN-13: 978-0-373-82799-2
ISBN-10:   0-373-82799-7

CALICO CHRISTMAS AT DRY CREEK

Copyright © 2008 by Janet Tronstad

www.SteepleHill.com

Printed in U.S.A.

In the beginning of time, it was said that

"…God created man in his own image,
in the image of God created he him…"

This was written in the Holy Bible,
the book of Genesis,
the second chapter, and the twenty-seventh verse.

And then, many generations later,
it was also said that

"God made me an Indian."

This was spoken by
Chief Sitting Bull
Lakota Medicine Man
1831–1890

This book is dedicated with love to my grandfather, Harold Norris, who loved nothing better than a good western novel. I wish he were alive to read this book.

Chapter One

Fort Keogh, Montana Territory, 1879

Elizabeth O'Brian heard voices outside her tent and thought it must be Mr. Miller coming to see if she was dead yet. It was a cold November day and she'd been sitting in her tent for eleven days now in this desolate land. It had only taken her husband, Matthew, and their baby, a few days to die from the fever so Elizabeth couldn't fault the blacksmith for being impatient.

"Mrs. O'Brian," a man's voice called in the distance.

Elizabeth ignored the voice. Mr. Miller knew she was still waiting for the fever to come upon her. He would just have to be patient a little longer. It wasn't as easy to die as it looked.

She supposed he was nervous because she was so close to the fort. No one had thought her tent would be here for this long. She had used the canvas from her wagon to make a tent in this slight ravine that stood a good fifty feet east of the mud-chinked logs that made up most of the buildings at Fort Keogh.

The canvas stretched from the back of her wagon to the only tree here, a squat cottonwood that had looked tired even before she'd tied her rope to it. She had made sure the tree put her far enough away from the fort to prevent the influenza from striking anyone there while at the same time still being close enough that Mr. Miller wouldn't have to walk far when he came to bury her.

The fort was a noisy, smelly place and Elizabeth wanted to die the way she had lived, quietly and alone.

"Mrs. O'Brian," the same man's voice called out. He was closer now.

She frowned. It didn't sound like Mr. Miller calling her.

She'd given the blacksmith her team of oxen in exchange for his promise to dig a proper burying hole for her next to the one that held Matthew and their baby, Rose. Once Mr. Miller had pledged himself, she believed he would do what was necessary when the time came. Still, she wanted her tent to be in sight of the man when it was time for him to do his job. She didn't want to give him any excuse to forget about the deal when she was no longer able to remind him of it. Men, she'd realized in her twenty-eight years on this earth, weren't always reliable.

Elizabeth got to her knees and crawled to the opening in the tent. She hadn't been out of the tent since dawn when she had gotten water from the barrel that was attached to the side of her wagon. She had added another piece of wood to the smoldering fire just outside her tent and boiled water for tea. Someone had left her a plate of hardtack biscuits yesterday. A morning frost had already covered the biscuits before she saw them, making them so brittle she had to dip each one in her tea before it was soft enough to chew. She'd had no appetite, but she'd forced herself to eat two of them for breakfast anyway.

After she ate, she had checked to see that the handkerchief was still securely tied around the back of the wagon seat. When she had refused to stay inside the fort, the doctor had insisted she have a signal for when the fever came upon her. She was to exchange the white handkerchief for a small piece of blue fabric at the first sign of heat. She'd ripped the cloth from the back of one of Matthew's shirts and had it, folded and ready for use, lying beside the old blankets on which she slept.

"Who is it?" Elizabeth peered through the canvas flap that was the closest thing to a door that she had. She saw two men standing a proper distance away. The canvas was stiff in her hands and still half-frozen from the night's cold. She could see her breath when she spoke.

Even with the white handkerchief up, the people who left food and firewood didn't try to speak to her. She had started leaving jars of her preserves on the wagon seat to repay them. She was always glad to see the jars were gone when she walked the few feet back to the wagon. She didn't want to be beholden to anyone when she died.

She wondered who wanted to talk with her now.

"Sergeant Rawlings, ma'am."

Elizabeth nodded. She had seen the man at the

blacksmith shop. "I'm sorry, but tell Mr. Miller that it's not time yet."

She moved the canvas in her hand slightly and felt the brush of a freezing wind. She tightened her blanket around her. She'd thought she'd never feel this kind of bitter cold again. Suddenly, she wondered if the blacksmith wanted more payment now that the temperatures were dropping, making it harder to dig in this gray dirt. She hoped not. A deal was a deal.

"We're not here about that. Could you come out here so we can talk?"

Elizabeth hadn't talked to anyone in days and she wasn't in a hurry to do so now. Besides, she wanted to study the men a little before she went out to meet them.

"Give me a minute."

She could see Sergeant Rawlings plainly, but the other man had his back to her. Initially, she thought he was one of the soldiers from the fort, too. But when she looked at him more closely, she realized he couldn't be a soldier. He wore a buckskin jacket and he had a black fur of some kind wrapped around his shoulders in a sling.

She shivered, and this time it was not from the cold. He must be an Indian. She'd seen Indian scouts coming and going from the fort, but this man looked like one of those wild Indians, the ones who killed people. She'd heard they did unspeakable things. Things she shouldn't even think about—like taking a lone woman's virtue and then, most likely, her scalp.

Elizabeth reached up to touch her hair. She suddenly wondered if Mr. Miller was planning to use the Indian to scare her into giving him more payment to dig her grave. Maybe Mr. Miller could threaten to have the Indian do the digging if she didn't cooperate. Her breath caught at the thought of a heathen preparing her grave.

Elizabeth kept count of the days, using a stick to mark their passage on the ground outside her tent. She should be in her grave by now, but she wasn't. She didn't know what was wrong. She supposed God was giving her more time on this earth in hopes she would repent of the anger she felt toward Him, but, if that was what He was doing, He might as well move things along. She knew who had taken her baby away from her and more time wouldn't change that.

She couldn't afford to lie in a grave dug by a heathen, though. What if God used that as an excuse to shut her out for all of eternity? She had been careful not to say a single word of complaint against God during this whole time—not to Matthew as he lay dying, not to the doctor, not to anyone—but an unholy grave might turn God from her anyway. She couldn't risk that; the only consolation she had left was the promise that she would see her baby again in Heaven.

She closed her eyes and tried to remember her exact words to the blacksmith, but she couldn't. Matthew had always said she didn't know how to drive a good bargain, and he was right. She should have made it clear to Mr. Miller that he was to handle the shovel himself. Over the past few days, she'd started to feel the cold seeping into the ground beneath her, but she hadn't realized what it might mean. She hoped God would let her die quickly before everything froze deep enough to trouble the blacksmith.

A horse neighed somewhere and Elizabeth opened her eyes again to look at the two men. Something was wrong. Maybe it wasn't Mr. Miller who wanted what was left of her possessions. Maybe it was the two men in front of her who were going to try and steal everything. They were certainly talking about something more serious than shovels as they waited for her. She swallowed. She would be no match for them if that's what they decided.

Elizabeth reached behind her for the old rifle she had, but then stopped. She couldn't shoot someone, not even if they were intent on stealing every last thing she owned.

She moved her hand and leaned forward to look more closely at the men. She did not see any sign of greed on the sergeant's face as he kept talking to the Indian. Neither one of them looked as if they were thinking of robbing her.

"It must be the preserves," Elizabeth suddenly muttered to herself in relief.

Of course, that was it. She'd forgotten they were in the wagon. The army man probably wanted the Indian to help him carry the rest of the preserves to the fort before the jars got so cold they cracked. Matthew had loaded the bottom of their wagon with things for the new store he planned to open, but Elizabeth had known she wouldn't be able to rely on Matthew to feed her and the baby, so she had canned everything she could before they left Kansas.

She'd even poured a mixture of beeswax and beef tallow on top of her jellies and apple butters so the ones they didn't eat on their journey would keep through the winter. Now, the last of the preserves were lying cradled on top of the woolens at the back of the wagon.

Well, she told herself after a moment, the sergeant had the right of it. Preserves were scarce out here. These soldiers lived on their rations of salt pork, dried beans and green coffee. She'd seen the men coming and going from the fort and none of them looked well-fed. She should have hauled all of those preserves up to the wagon seat before now, anyway. Even her pickled things, like her red beets and sour cabbage, shouldn't go to waste just because she was dying.

It wasn't until the man in the buckskin moved that Elizabeth saw the Indian girl sitting on the pinto pony near the fort. She must be about nine or ten years old and she had a blanket wrapped around her. Edges of a faded calico dress showed through where the blanket didn't cover and animal pelts were tied around her legs. Elizabeth couldn't imagine why the girl was watching them so intently.

"Could you just come out here, please?" Sergeant Rawlings called out again.

Really—men, Elizabeth thought to herself. She supposed it never occurred to any of them to let her die in peace and worry about the preserves later. That was men for you. Always thinking about their stomachs. Matthew had been like that, too. He had always expected her to have a meal ready even when he didn't provide her with a scrap of meat or a handful of flour to use in the making of it.

But, oh, how she missed him and Rose. Matthew hadn't been much of a provider, but he had treated her well enough. She had been learning to please him, too, and, if they'd been given a little more time together, she was sure she would have succeeded in making him happy with their marriage. He was the first family that was really her own. And he'd given her Rose. Her baby only had to be herself to melt everyone's heart.

Elizabeth wrapped a blanket around her like a shawl and stepped out of the tent. The ground outside was slippery from frost and she felt the cold deeply as she walked toward the sergeant and the Indian. She had taken several steps when the man in the buckskin turned around and she saw him fully for the first time.

"Oh, dear, I'm sorry." She stopped and stared. Why, he wasn't an Indian at all. His eyes were blue and the skin around his eyes, the part that was wrinkled from squinting, was undeniably white. His nose wasn't flat like some of the Indians she'd seen and his cheekbones were high. Even with that knowledge, though, she wasn't quite sure about him. Up close, he seemed larger than she had expected. And more fierce than a white man should be. He looked like a warrior no matter what color he was.

"There's no need to apologize," Sergeant Rawlings said stiffly. "We're sorry to trouble you."

Elizabeth nodded and tried to think of something to say to cover the erratic beating of her heart. "It's no bother. It just took me a while because—because I wasn't prepared for company."

She was still staring at the other man. She'd never had this kind of breathless reaction to the sight of anyone. Of course, it probably wasn't really the sight of him that was causing her heart to continue racing. It was only that she had thought he was a savage capable of doing anything.

Even now that Elizabeth knew the man she was looking at was a white man, she was still uneasy around him. He was nothing at all like Matthew. Nothing like any man she'd ever seen before.

Oh, dear—whatever he was, he was looking straight at her and frowning.

Then he spoke. "There must be some mistake. She doesn't look like a widow—just look at her."

Elizabeth had expected his voice to be harsh, but it wasn't. It sounded kind and, if she was hearing right, a little discouraged. Although why the man would be feeling that way was beyond her. If he was worried about the way anyone around here looked, he should be worrying about himself instead of her. The soldiers here dressed better than he did. And that wasn't saying much.

She'd noticed right off that the dye in the men's uniforms was poor and some patches of wool were a darker blue than others. The buttonholes were fraying, too. That's what came of using indigo for dye; everyone knew it ate away at the cloth. She would have used dyer's woad if she'd been charged with making the garments, although the leaves of the plant did take longer to prepare.

Even with all of that, though, none of the soldiers wore buckskin the way this man did. One army man she'd talked to said he'd gladly wear a buffalo coat in winter if he had one, but he'd rather wear the blanket from his bed than dress like an Indian.

Elizabeth looked at the man in buckskin. The furs the man wore over his shoulder formed a pack of some sort that he kept close to his chest.

Elizabeth let the blanket she wore as a shawl slip away from her. The air chilled her skin, but she didn't want to feel she was hiding anything. In her childhood, she had learned that a soft answer would smooth away most unpleasantness and that she was the one always expected to give it.

"Please, don't let my appearance concern you. I normally do better," she said.

The wind blew a strand of brown hair across her cheek and Elizabeth knew what the men saw. The mosquito bites on her face had faded, but the freckles she'd gotten from neglecting to wear her sunbonnet on the dreadful journey here were still plain. By now, the icy wind would have drawn all of the other color from her face, as well, so the freckles would stand out like tiny pebbles scattered on a bank of fresh snow.

And she still wasn't wearing a hat; the only one she owned was that worn-out yellow sunbonnet and she refused to wear it ever again. She might even burn it in the fire one night before she died. Everything about it reminded her of the journey here and she wanted no part of those memories.

Elizabeth lifted her head high. She'd grown weary of trying to please others. She'd been orphaned young and spent her childhood being passed from household to household whenever extra help was needed. She'd never been asked to sit at the family table in any of these places where she worked, but she'd earned a measure of respect with her cooking and with her clever ways of dyeing cloth.

She was wearing her best dress, even if there was dirt on her skirt after crawling to the opening in her tent. Her hands brushed at the folds of the gray silk garment that she'd been given by the last family she had worked for. It had been damaged when they had given it to her, of course, but it was still the only silk dress she was likely to ever own. And it was twilled silk. Elizabeth had put the dress on last week when she realized she could hardly expect Mr. Miller to change her clothes for her burial.

"I never said there was anything wrong with the way you look." The man's eyes softened. "I just expected someone older. And not so pretty."

Elizabeth watched in horror as the man reached out and touched her chin as through she was a child to be consoled.

"I'm hardly pretty," Elizabeth said, a little more sharply than she intended. She moved her face slightly to discourage him, although his touch on her chin had been gentle and, surprisingly, pleasant.

She'd heard enough warnings in her life to know handsome men couldn't always be trusted, especially not when they were talking to females who had no protectors. And this man was certainly trying to turn her up sweet for some purpose of his own. Matthew once said she looked nice, but that wasn't the same as saying she was pretty. No one ever called her pretty and Elizabeth was sensible enough to know not to expect it. It wasn't true.

She wondered for a moment if the man was delusional and then she remembered the fever. She always did look better when her cheeks had some color in them. Maybe the fever was already on her and she just hadn't noticed it. She put her hand to her forehead.

"Well, I can't expect you to help me." The buckskin man finally said before turning to the sergeant as though he hadn't just been smiling at her. "There's got to be someone else."

Elizabeth was ready to leave when the sergeant spoke urgently. "There's nobody else. You've got to ask her—for the baby's sake."

"What—" Elizabeth looked around. Her hand dropped away from her forehead. There was no fever heat unless, of course, she was the one who was delusional. "What baby?"

There were no babies at the fort. She had asked. Mr. Miller thought she wanted to save herself the pain of seeing a living baby, but that wasn't it. Babies were so innocent. If there was a baby around she would have asked to look at it, from a distance, of course, so as not to risk giving the fever to the little one.

She saw the buckskin man's hand go to the bundle he wore across his chest.

"This baby," the man said.

"Ohhh. Can I see it?"

The man started to turn the bundle toward her.

"I'll keep back so you won't have to worry about it getting sick."

The man stopped his turning and looked up at the soldier. "I thought you said she didn't have the fever."

"That's right," Sergeant Rawlings said and then looked at Elizabeth. "The doctor said you'd be dead by now if you were going to get it. I was just coming over to tell you that when I ran into Jake here."

"We can't always time our deaths perfectly," Elizabeth said. It wasn't up to the doctor when she died. "I'm sure I'll die soon enough."

"But you don't have the fever now?" the buckskin man asked.

"No, not yet, Mr….ah…Mr.…"

"It's just Jake," the man said.

Elizabeth frowned. After he had touched her chin, she should have known he had no manners. If she could be courteous when she was dying, the man could at least be polite when he stood there in vigorous health. He might dress like a heathen, but he didn't need to act like one. A full name was not too much of an introduction to ask.

"How long do you plan to wait for this fever?" Jake asked.

Elizabeth lifted her chin. If he wasn't going to show her the baby, he could just say so. And he could keep his hands to himself. "I'm sure I don't know Mr.…"

She didn't know why she bothered with the man's manners. She just wanted him to relent and show her the baby. She'd love to see a baby.

Jake was looking at her impatiently. "If you need the full name to feel better, it's Jake Hargrove."

"Well, Mr. Hargrove." Elizabeth nodded her head in acknowledgment. There. That had made her feel better. "I'm Elizabeth O'Brian and I plan to be here as long as it takes to die. Did you need this land for something?"

It wasn't only the preserves that might interest the men, Elizabeth had realized. They could also want the very ground under her feet. God might not even leave her with that.

Except for the lone cottonwood tree, the piece of ground where she had her tent didn't have anything on it, not after she'd pulled up the few scraggly thistles that had managed to survive the scorching heat of this past summer. There were more cottonwood trees farther up the ravine, but she doubted even a jackrabbit wanted the barren piece of land that was now her camp. Although she did know there were men who would lay claim to something just because someone else had their tent pitched on it already. Maybe this buckskin man was one of them.

"No, no, it's not that," Jake said and then he hesitated. "It's you. Women are scarce out here and it's hard for a man to find one when he needs her."

Elizabeth blinked. "I beg your pardon."

Sergeant Rawlings spoke up. "It's not what you think, ma'am. It's on account of the baby being hungry is all."

"Oh." Elizabeth breathed out in wonder. She knew in that moment she was going to see the baby.

Jake hesitated and then finished unwinding the furs from his shoulders.

The baby was so tiny and its eyes were shut. Elizabeth thought it must be sleeping until the baby opened its mouth and yawned. Her Rose used to yawn like that.

"There's no one to feed her," Jake said. "I asked all around Miles City before I came out to the fort."

"Miller thought he might be able to milk one of your oxen," Sergeant Rawlings said. "But it didn't seem like it would work."

"I should think not," Elizabeth said as she stepped closer to the baby. She left enough room so that she wouldn't pass on any sickness just in case. "It's a little girl then, is it? If I could, I would feed her."

The baby started to give a weak wail.

Elizabeth felt her breasts grow heavy with milk. "Where's her mother?"

"Dead," Jake said flatly and then repeated what the soldier had said, "The doctor says you're not going to get the fever." He looked square at her. "You're her last hope. She'll die without something to eat."

"But still…" Elizabeth knew she would not have let anyone who might come down with the fever touch her Rose. This baby here was frail and reminded her of how Rose had been when she was dying. If Elizabeth closed her eyes, she could still see the image of Rose lying so still after she took her last breath.

Suddenly, the baby stopped its wail.

"I can't…" Elizabeth started to say, but her arms were already reaching out.

God would have to forgive her if that doctor was wrong, because she couldn't let this baby die without trying to help it.

Jake held out the baby. Elizabeth wrapped a corner of her blanket around it and bent down to go back inside her tent. She supposed the two men would just stand outside and wait, but she didn't care. She had a baby to hold again.

Once they got started, Elizabeth was surprised at how easily the baby fell into the rhythm of nursing. Even when the baby had finished eating, Elizabeth just sat there for a while with the baby at her breast. The little one's hair was black and soft. She was an Indian baby, of course, but she looked like Rose all the same.

The baby didn't seem as heathen as a warrior would, though.

She had heard that some of the white men who came to the territories took Indian wives. She wondered briefly if Jake Hargrove had married the baby's mother in a church ceremony.

For a moment, Elizabeth was glad Matthew wasn't here to see her nursing the infant. From the day he had proposed to her, Elizabeth had tried to be the wife Matthew had wanted. He had married beneath himself; there was no question of that. A lady would never nurse another's baby and Elizabeth felt sure Matthew would refuse to let her do so if he were here, especially because the baby was not white. And probably irregular in its birth, as well.

The sun was almost setting when Elizabeth opened

the tent flap again. Sergeant Rawlings had gone, but the other man was still there sitting on the ground near her wagon. The Indian girl had come closer to the wagon, as well, even though she still sat on top of her pony.

When she opened the tent flap, Jake stood up and walked over to her.

"What's the baby's name?" Elizabeth asked as she knelt at the door of her tent and lifted the baby up to the man.

"She doesn't have a name yet." Jake took the baby and began to wrap it back into the furs he wore over his shoulder.

"Oh, surely she has a name," Elizabeth said as she stood up and hugged her blanket around her. Hoping for a girl, she and Matthew had picked out the name Rose before their baby was even born. Rose had been the name of Matthew's mother, but Elizabeth had liked the name for its own sake, too. "She'll sleep for now."

"The Lakota wait to name their babies," Jake said as he adjusted the baby inside his makeshift sling. "She hadn't earned her name yet when she was brought to me."

"My sister will be called the Crying One," the girl on the pony said. "For the tears of her people."

Elizabeth was surprised to hear the girl speaking English. Her words were not easily formed, but Elizabeth could understand what she was saying.

"Your sister doesn't belong to the Lakota anymore," Jake said. "She belongs to the people of her grandfather."

The girl didn't say anything. She just sat, facing east. She didn't even seem to look at the man. Her face was smooth, devoid of expression.

Elizabeth had heard arguments like this before.

"Your dress is beautiful." Elizabeth smiled up just in case the girl looked over at her. The faded yellow tones of the calico looked almost white in the rays of the setting sun. A good boiling with some of the dried marigold petals Elizabeth had in her wagon would bring the color back, though. "Your sister is fortunate to have a big sister like you to take care of her."

"I cannot take care of her." The girl turned and looked at Elizabeth for the first time. "She needs you."

"Oh."

Elizabeth saw the girl's face crumble. Resentment and pleading both shone in the young girl's eyes. How she must hate asking for help. And how desperately she wanted it.

Elizabeth nodded. "Of course, I—I will do what I can until some other way is found."

"What other way is there?" Jake asked. His voice was strained, too. "The baby sickens on cow's milk. I tried to buy some of that canned milk in Miles City—the kind they gave our men in the war—but none of the stores sell it. Most of them hadn't even heard of it. You are our only hope."

If things had been different, she and Matthew might have eventually owned a store like the ones that the man mentioned. That had been Matthew's dream. They probably wouldn't have canned milk, either, at least not in the beginning. But, in time, who knew?

Matthew always said he would tend the store while Elizabeth tended Rose. He had all those things in the wagon to sell. A fierce sadness rose up in Elizabeth just thinking about it. Those dreams and hopes were all dead. It didn't seem fair that the peace of her passing should be disturbed with memories of things that would never come true. Matthew had died so fast, he hadn't even had time to mourn his lost dreams.

Death had been taking its time with her, though. Without her Rose, she wanted to die. She had no family and she would not go back to being an outsider in other people's homes. She was ready to die. She did not need two pairs of eyes watching her and demanding that she stay alive. She wished she could just close her eyes and keep them closed until she was done with this life.

But, Elizabeth admitted, the doctor in the fort had been a cautious man when he treated Matthew and Rose. A professional man like that wasn't likely to make a mistake about the fever. She wondered if the doctor had seen the Indian baby. Elizabeth knew most people wouldn't think it was a tragedy if one more heathen baby died, but she found she did. She had nursed this one. This baby reminded her of Rose. She wanted it to live.

"Of course, I will do what I can," Elizabeth finally said. She looked over at the baby, snug in the man's arms. "But if the doctor is wrong and the fever comes, you must leave. If you stay, the baby will die anyway."

Elizabeth knew she could not bear to watch another baby die. Surely there were limits to what God could ask of any person, even of her.

Chapter Two

It was night when Jake Hargrove returned from the fort and laid himself down on his buffalo robe. He was bone tired. He'd stood off Indian raids and packs of starving wolves, but he'd never been more worried than he was now. He had no idea how to keep the baby alive if this Mrs. O'Brian wouldn't stay with him through the winter. The men he'd talked to inside hadn't been encouraging; they'd said she was one powerfully stubborn woman and she was set on dying.

Still, for now, she was doing what she could for his niece, Jake told himself. And a woman needed to be stubborn to survive in this land so he didn't begrudge her that. He just needed to turn her mind around to match his. That was all.

He could see her tent clearly in the moonlight from where he lay. He'd put his bed a few yards from it. The baby was sleeping inside the tent with the woman and Spotted Fawn was lying next to the wagon, close enough so she would hear if her sister cried. The two girls hadn't slept that far apart since Red Tail, his half brother, had brought them to him, begging him to raise his daughters in the white man's world so they would live.

Jake had accepted the girls, knowing there was no other way for them. Sitting Bull and the rest of the Lakota Sioux were starving in Canada. Once Red Tail had said goodbye to his daughters, he had gone back to do what he could for the rest of his tribe. He told Jake not to expect to see him again in this life.

Jake put his rifle next to him on the ground. He'd checked earlier and seen that the woman had a rifle in her tent, as well. It had to be the one the blacksmith said he'd given her when she refused to stay inside the fort, claiming the noise and dirt were troublesome to her.

When Jake first heard about the woman, he was surprised no one had made her go into Miles City and take a room at the new hotel there. The bare land around here was no place for a woman from the East. The town was on the other side of the Tongue River, but it was only a few miles away from here.

Of course, now he knew the men at the fort had tried to reason with her. When Jake had talked to the blacksmith, Mr. Miller had said it was all he could do to get the woman to promise that she would run to the fort if she heard a warning shot being fired. The blacksmith didn't look Jake in the eye when he told him that. They both knew a raiding party could be so quiet there would be no warning shot, at least not one that would do the woman any good.

Not all of the Sioux had fled to Canada after their battle with General Custer. Some of the younger braves were still in the territories, their hearts set on vengeance and thievery. As determined as they were to kill all of the white people they could find, these renegades were also looking for extra horses. That was one reason why Jake kept his rifle close. The easiest place to find horses was to rob an army corral, which meant they would need to come to the fort. Once the raiding party got to the fort, the loaded wagon standing outside would be a temptation. As would the woman inside the tent.

Jake shook his head just thinking about that woman. She should be sitting in a parlor back East somewhere. He didn't know what her husband had been thinking to bring her out here; she didn't belong in a land like this. But, as surely as Jake knew she didn't belong, he wasn't going to suggest she go back. Now that she was here, he was going to ask her to stay with him for the winter.

She likely hadn't faced up to it yet, but she had a problem as big as his. She couldn't winter where she was. The winds from the north had been damp lately and that meant winter would come early and it would bring enough snow to bury that makeshift tent of hers. At least, she would be warm and dry if she was with him and the girls.

Unfortunately, for the woman to stay with them, Jake would need to marry her. He'd known that before he met her. Miles City was an unforgiving place these days and he had the girls to consider. They were already viewed with suspicion because of the color of their skin. They would be true outcasts if people found out he was not married to the woman living with them. And, there would be no way to keep the woman a secret. He'd be a fool to even try.

Of course, when he'd first heard of the widow, he'd assumed she would be older and practical enough to make an arrangement with him. Jake looked up at the sky searching for stars. He hadn't counted on Mrs. O'Brian being young or having eyes that made him want to protect her from things he didn't even see.

The truth was he couldn't even protect her from the things he could see coming. He and the girls were going to have a battle finding acceptance in Miles City and any woman he married would be in the battle with them. There was no limit to the mean-spiritedness of human beings and Jake figured his little family was going to see their share of it this winter.

It made him weary just thinking of it. If he had a fire going, he would read some from the Bible his mother had given him as a boy. It never failed to comfort him. His mother had been a fine lady. Of course, she'd been totally unsuited to the roughness of life out here. He relaxed just thinking of his old home, hidden on the side of a mountain northwest of here by the pines growing thick and tall all around. His father had brought them there, not believing the reports he'd heard that the trapping days were almost over. He thought it was all just rumors spread by the Hudson's Bay Company. He pictured getting rich on furs once the other trappers gave up, but he barely managed to feed his family.

Jake had grieved when his mother died a couple of
years after they came West. The crude cabin where they
lived seemed to shrink and grow empty without her. He
and his father never talked about his mother after her
death. They had both felt too guilty for failing her. His
father hadn't even put a marker on her burial place. The
last thing Jake had done, before he left to go out on his
own, was to find a smooth slab of rock and place it in front
of his mother's grave with her name scratched on it.

By that time, his father had married again, this time
to a Lakota squaw. Red Tail was their son.

If he didn't have the girls, Jake would not consider
marriage—especially not to a woman like Elizabeth
O'Brian. She reminded him too much of his mother. This
land had changed in the almost forty years he'd lived
here, but it still wasn't a place for pretty, young white
women. He didn't want to watch another one of them
grow bitter and fade away here. He didn't have much
choice, though. Not if he wanted to keep the baby alive.

Elizabeth wasn't sure if it was the pebble under her
back or the smell of frying salt pork that woke her the
next morning. She could see out the flap in her tent well
enough to know there were heavy gray clouds hanging
low in the sky. There was also a biting cold to the
morning air. Winter was coming. The low bluffs in the
distance might even have snow on top of them by now.

Elizabeth hadn't slept well and it was later than she'd
planned to waken. It had taken her hours last night to
coax the older girl close enough to the tent so that Eliza-

beth wouldn't worry about her. Finally, Spotted Fawn had agreed to sleep beside her tent when Elizabeth said she might need help with the baby.

Fortunately, the baby only stirred twice during the night. Elizabeth had fed her both times and the little one was doing better. Maybe this man, Jake, would be content to spend a few more days near the fort so Elizabeth could nurse the baby. That should give him enough time to find someone else to take care of the infant.

In the cold light of morning, Elizabeth accepted the fact that she was going to live. She looked down at the sleeping infant. Maybe God was keeping her alive to save this Indian baby. That was the only thing that made sense, even though she couldn't help but wonder why He saw fit to worry about this little one when He had not hesitated to take her Rose away.

Elizabeth knew no one was supposed to question the ways of God, but she couldn't help her thoughts. It would be a wondrous, as well as a bitter thing, if God used her to save this heathen child's life when she had not been able to do anything but watch her own baby die.

Unfortunately, no matter what her thoughts, she could not spend her day hiding inside her tent. Whether or not she wanted to see him again, Jake Hargrove was out there and he'd naturally want to know about the baby.

Elizabeth pulled the blankets closer to the sleeping infant before she tried to smooth back her hair. Maybe she could slip around to the wagon without being seen and get her mirror. She didn't want anyone accusing her of being untidy again. Maybe if she rubbed her cheeks with a damp cloth, the color on her face would even out, as well.

When Elizabeth opened the flaps to her tent, she could see that Jake wasn't the one frying the pork. There was a layer of frost on the ground and someone had hollowed out a place in the dirt to build a cooking fire, even though the blackened ashes from her own fire were only a few feet away.

Elizabeth didn't recognize the man who crouched by the fire's coals, although he was wearing the usual army uniform so he clearly belonged to the fort. She took a quick look at the ground around him and didn't see any signs of his belongings. She did see that the man had a coffeepot settled at the edge of the fire and was heating a rock that looked as if it had some biscuits warming on it.

She took a deep breath. The coffee didn't have the faintly bitter smell of green coffee, either. That's what she usually smelled around the fort. No, this was the kind of coffee a man would buy special in the mercantile. That soldier had probably been hoarding that bit of coffee for months. And now he was celebrating something.

Elizabeth frowned. The only thing around here to celebrate was his new camp. Why—she drew in her breath as she finally understood. That man wanted her place. Elizabeth's needs had been pushed aside by others all of her life, and she'd accepted it. But now that she'd been cheated out of death too, something rose up inside of her. She refused to be pushed any longer. She didn't care what her hair looked like.

"This spot's taken," Elizabeth said as she stepped out of her tent. The canvas had kept the frost away from the ground inside, but the icy cold outside made her gasp when her foot touched the ground. She had worn a hole in her left shoe from all of the walking she'd done on the way here and the cold went right through her stocking. She saw her breath come out in white puffs again today.

But she ignored all of that. As cold as she was on the outside, she felt a growing heat inside. For all this man knew, she was still dying. People needed to wait for the dead to be finished with their business before they took everything from them. She liked the spot where she was camped; she intended to keep it.

"If you're planning to set up a camp, you might try a little farther down the ravine. There are more cotton-woods and dry thistle down there anyway so it will be easier for fires and all." Elizabeth forced herself to smile. If she stood in one place, the ground under her shoes grew a little warmer.

"I'm not setting up camp." The man stood up indignantly. His nose was red from the chill of the morning and his hair was slicked back with some kind of grease. He looked vaguely familiar. "I'm cooking you breakfast."

"Me?" Elizabeth was astonished. She forgot all about her manners and her cold feet. "Whatever for?"

What would possess the man to do something like that? No one had ever cooked breakfast for her, not even the morning after she'd given birth to Rose. Maybe the doctor had decided she was going to die after all and this soldier had been sent to prepare her last meal. Really, that was no way to break the news to a person.

"Who told you to cook me breakfast? That doctor?"

"Nobody told me to do it. I just know women like to have breakfast cooked for them once in a while."

The man smiled, even though he didn't look too happy.

Elizabeth took a closer look at him. The man had shaved this morning. It wasn't Sunday. Outside of God's day, the men at the fort only shaved for special occasions like Christmas, the occasional dance and, of course—funerals.

She swore she'd never listen to a doctor again. The man couldn't even keep a proper log of days. He had probably lost track of time and, when he recalculated, discovered his error.

"I'm still dying, aren't I? Just tell me the truth. I won't make a fuss."

Elizabeth braced herself even though it was what she had suspected all along.

"No one's dying. The doctor told me you were as healthy today as you've ever been in your life."

Elizabeth wasn't really listening to the man anymore. She was looking around. The man cooking breakfast wasn't the only soldier here. There were actually several soldiers standing to the left of her. They'd been hidden from her view when she was in the tent. They were certainly standing quietly. And they all seemed to be carrying big, tall bunches of dried weeds.

"Is something wrong?" Elizabeth asked. Surely, the

men would be worrying about their rifles and not those weeds if something was really wrong.

The first man in the line stepped forward. The gold penny buttons on his uniform were all in place and his posture was straight. He'd recently shaved, as well. She could tell that by the whiteness of his skin where his beard had once been.

Surely the doctor wouldn't lie about whether she was expected to live.

"I was hoping you'd like these flowers," the man said as he handed her what looked like dried cottontails. Then he took a deep breath and recited something he'd obviously memorized. "They should be roses to match the roses in your cheeks."

The man gave an abrupt bow and turned to the side.

"But Rose is—" Elizabeth swallowed. She hadn't even said the name aloud since Rose died. She'd scratched it in the dirt several times when her longing had overcome her, but she'd never spoken it again until now. "That's my daughter's name."

The men weren't listening.

"Roses aren't fair enough to compare to your loveliness," the second man said as he thrust another bunch of weeds in her direction. At least, he'd had the foresight to tuck in a little sage so it smelled better. "I'm saving to buy some land when I finish up here at the fort. I've got prospects. This is going to be cattle country soon. You'll see."

The third man stepped forward.

Elizabeth finally realized what was happening. "You can't be here *courting* me."

She wouldn't have been more surprised if they had shown up to tar and feather her. She supposed it was flattering, but— "I'm afraid there's been some misunderstanding. I'm not—that is, my husband and my baby, Rose—they're, well…"

Elizabeth gave up and pointed. Surely they could see the mound of fresh dirt near the edge of the ravine. She had carried over the biggest rock she could find to mark the place so the grave wouldn't be lost in the vast expanse of land here. But now that she looked again, it didn't seem as if it would be enough. The weather here would wear the rock down or someone would move it not knowing what it was.

The third man took off his hat. "It's sorry I am for your loss, but I was hoping you'd be willing to be my wife."

"Your wife! But I don't even know you."

Never, in all of the years that Elizabeth had longed for a family, had she imagined that a man she didn't even know would want to marry her. It didn't seem quite decent, somehow. Matthew had taken her to church for months before he proposed. That was the way civilized men courted their wives.

Elizabeth hadn't seen Jake coming toward her until he was suddenly there. The sight of him, standing so solid before her was reassuring. He might have surprised her yesterday, but today he felt like safety itself. At least he could explain that she was not looking for a husband.

"Tell them," Elizabeth said to Jake. She could hardly think of what to say so she just gestured to the men.

"You're going about it all wrong," Jake said to the

men. "She sets a great deal of importance to names. You might want to introduce yourself before you propose."

"Well, it takes more than a name to—" Elizabeth stopped as she looked up at Jake for the first time. "Surely no one expects me to get married *now*."

Elizabeth didn't know what to do. Maybe Jake didn't understand the problem completely. She was going to explain it, but she noticed he had changed out of his buckskins and stood before her in a blue shirt and black wool pants. It didn't seem right that the blue dye of the shirt should match his eyes so exactly. And, the color was evenly spread so she knew someone had used dyer's woad to get the blue. It had probably been one of those big factories that dyed the cloth, but it was the same process and it looked good. Not that the man probably knew anything about how his shirt was made. Men never did.

Elizabeth noticed her breathing was betraying her again as she looked at him. She realized she was actually gawking at the man.

"I could still be dying," she finally muttered and then turned to face the soldiers. It wasn't all she'd meant to say, but that piece of information alone should put the men off the idea of marriage. "The doctor could be wrong. It's a bad death—influenza. I'd probably pass it along to any man I…ah…married."

There. Elizabeth crossed her arms. She'd said enough. She'd be left in peace.

Jake should have realized what would happen. He'd gone to beg some hot water off the blacksmith so he could shave again without needing to build a fire and, when he had gotten back, he'd seen the men. He wouldn't have taken so long, but he had a new razor strap and he felt a wedding proposal deserved a careful shave. While he was gone, the men had gathered.

He knew right away what that meant. It hadn't taken long for word to get around that the woman was going to live. There weren't many women at the fort and it wasn't often an opportunity to marry presented itself to these soldiers. If the men hadn't been so scared of the fever, they would have been lined up to court Elizabeth before now.

Jake couldn't blame them for taking any chance they could. He knew how tired a man got of his own company. He just wished they were not lining up for this particular woman. Jake could see the men looking at each other and wondering if the doctor really had miscalculated how long it would take for someone to come down with the fever.

"I can't marry one of them," Elizabeth said as she turned to Jake. Her eyes were wide. "I've never even seen most of them until this morning. They're absolute strangers."

Jake wished he could ease the panic he saw in Elizabeth's eyes, but he knew he wasn't going to. "Given that you've known me a bit longer, maybe you should marry me instead."

She just stared at him as if she hadn't heard him right. Jake figured he better add some more persuasion. "You're going to have to do something before winter comes anyway."

Jake could hear Elizabeth's breathing as she consid-ered his words. He'd heard the same shallow breaths from wild horses that had been corralled for the first time. He would have put his hand on her arm to soothe her, but he thought it would have done the opposite.

"But what if she does get sick?" one of the soldiers called out. "You'd likely die, too, if you married her."

"I'm not worried. She looks healthy enough to me. And pretty, too."

Ah, good, he thought. She wasn't looking so scared now that she was a bit angry again. He found it hard to believe Elizabeth was a widow when she blushed up pink the way she was doing.

"They're right. If the doctor's wrong, I could be dying any day now," Elizabeth said. Jake thought she sounded downright hopeful. "You need someone else for your daughters."

"They're my nieces, not my daughters."

"Oh."

"The doctor's not wrong," he said. She looked so troubled that he decided to reach out to touch her arm anyway; he only pulled back when he saw her move away. "If you're waiting to see if you get the fever, you could wait just as easy if you are a married woman."

"I *am* a married woman. At least, I—I was."

Jake nodded. He'd expected that. She was still in love with her husband. Well, it was probably better that way. All he really needed was someone for the girls. "I'm not asking for myself. It's for the baby."

"I don't need to marry you to help with the baby. Of course I'll help with the baby."

Jake nodded. That was something. "I can't keep the girls here at the fort all winter, though. We have to go back to my place and folks won't understand us living under the same roof and not being married."

Jake didn't add that the girls wouldn't be welcome at the fort. The only Indians at the fort were the Crow scouts and the Sioux who were here against their will. The girls would be treated like captives and he couldn't do that to them. They would have a hard time gaining acceptance with civilians; but they would have no hope of finding it among the soldiers and their families. The girls' tribe had fought General Custer and his men. No army man would forget that defeat soon.

"I could take my tent with me," Elizabeth said.

"You would need to be with the baby at night. The baby can't sleep in your tent when it gets colder." He wondered if the woman had any idea what winters were like here.

Elizabeth nodded. "Still, we don't need to get married."

"The people of Miles City will see it differently."

"I don't care about gossip."

"Neither do I, but Spotted Fawn needs to go to school."

"Ah." Elizabeth nodded.

She still didn't look convinced. And she was looking at him as though there was something lacking in him.

Jake had known a woman from back East would have a hard time with the land out here. But he'd never quite considered that she might have an even harder time with him. He'd changed out of his buckskins, but he knew he didn't look like what an Eastern woman would expect in a husband. Well, he decided, it was best she know the truth about him.

Jake wasn't the man his mother had hoped he would grow up to be. He didn't much care for big cities. Or small ones, either. He was wearing wool now, but he preferred buckskin. Still, he was a fair-minded man and he didn't expect more in a bargain than someone should have to give. "It can just be a piece of paper between us. All I need is someone for the baby."

She was silent.

"My girls, they're good girls."

"Oh, I'm sure they are."

Jake could see he wasn't making progress. Her eyes still seemed drawn to that grave, as if she was afraid the ones who were dead and under the ground could hear what she was saying and would rise up to accuse her of disloyalty.

"It wouldn't need to be a real marriage," Jake made his words even clearer. "You'll be able to get it annulled in the spring if you want."

He'd do whatever she wanted in that regard.

Elizabeth just stood there looking sad. "I just buried my husband. I don't need another one."

As a boy, Jake had watched his father trading pelts. Everyone, no matter their tribe, had something they wanted. A good trader just watched until he figured out what that was. It didn't take long to figure out what Elizabeth really wanted.

"I can make you a marker for that grave if you agree to help me. We can get a good-sized piece of granite sent down from Fort Benton. It'll last forever."

Elizabeth was looking at him now.

"I'm a pretty good carver. I'll set their names on it and anything else you want to say. There won't be a fancier headstone in the whole territory." It was the best he could do.

"Oh." Elizabeth breathed out. "Matthew would like that, but—"

"And an angel. I could carve an angel on the corner of it for your daughter."

Jake hadn't carved anything but letters on his mother's stone. But he whittled some in the evenings and he'd carved shapes of most of the animals around here. He could do an angel.

Elizabeth just stood there, blinking.

"Don't cry," Jake said.

"I never cry," Elizabeth whispered and then took a deep breath. "You have yourself a deal."

Now it was Jake's turn to be surprised into silence.

"You can't marry him," one of the soldiers in line protested. "I haven't had a chance to read you my poetry. I wrote a poem for you and everything."

Elizabeth turned to the soldiers in line and squared her shoulders. "I'm sorry. I haven't thanked any of you properly. You've paid me a great compliment. I'm honored, of course. Could I give you each a jar of sweet pickles? I canned them myself."

"Well, that'd be nice of you," the soldier who had

removed his hat said. "I haven't had anything like that since I was back home."

Jake helped Elizabeth hand out four jars of pickles.

After the soldiers left the campsite, Elizabeth turned to Jake. "This marriage—it's only for the baby?"

"I'll bunk down in the lean-to and give the rest of the place to you and the girls."

Elizabeth nodded. "I gave Mr. Miller my oxen in exchange for his promise to bury me when the time comes so—well—I expect him to do what he said. Even if he has to come to your place and get me."

"You don't need Mr. Miller now. You have me."

"Oh." Elizabeth looked at him skeptically. "Are you a God-fearing man, Mr. Hargrove?"

Jake was a little taken back. "Yes."

She still looked suspicious. "The God of the Bible?"

Jake smiled. "Yes."

"Well, then…" She paused as though weighing his words. "Do you promise to dig the burying hole yourself?"

"If that's what you want."

"I don't want any easy promises here. I know I can't come back and make sure you've done that particular job properly so I'd be relying on your word. I want you to dig the hole yourself and do it with prayer in your heart."

"You've got my word." Jake had seen peace pipes passed with less resolve than Elizabeth showed. "I'll take care of you in good times and bad times. Dead or alive."

"When I go, I'll want to be buried beside my baby."

"I'll see to it. I'll even leave room on the headstone for all three of you."

Elizabeth nodded. "Then I think we should ask for the oxen back."

Jake knew a battle could be lost if a man didn't act quickly to secure his victory. "I'll get the oxen and then we'll head out. I know the minister in Miles City. The Reverend Olson. He'll say the words for us."

"Matthew and I never did get as far as Miles City. But I heard they had a fine preacher there. Mr. Miller promised to ask the man to come and say a few words over my grave when I—you know—" Elizabeth nodded to the grave "—when I died—which I guess isn't going to be as soon as I thought."

Elizabeth pressed her lips together firmly.

Jake hoped that meant she was accepting her new life. "The reverend's a good man."

"If we're going to see him about getting married, I'd like to have some time alone with him before I take my vows."

Jake figured that meant she wasn't accepting her new life at all. She was probably going to ask the minister about her funeral. He didn't know what the Reverend Olson would think when Jake rode into town with a bride who was more intent on her funeral than she was on getting married to him.

Of course, she probably wouldn't be content with just talking to the reverend about her worries. She might mention it to anyone who would listen until finally even the old trappers would hear about it. They'd have a fine time telling about the woman who'd rather go to her own funeral than marry up with Jake Hargrove.

Oh, well, Jake told himself with a wry grin; he never was one to begrudge others a good laugh around their evening fires. He just hoped they got a few things straight. Like the fact that his bride's eyes were some of the most beautiful eyes a man was likely to see this side of the Missouri. He hadn't expected that. They reminded him of the moss that grew on the side of those ponderosa pines high in the mountains where he'd lived as a boy.

Being married, even temporarily, to a woman with eyes like that couldn't be all bad. He'd just have to think of ways to keep her happy until she decided to leave. Even his mother had taken a few months to judge this land before she decided that she hated it. His mother might have gone longer before making her decision if she'd had something to distract her. Women always liked new clothes. Maybe he should buy the woman a new dress to match those eyes of hers.

And a pretty brooch. His mother had set great store by her few jewels. Jake stopped himself. He wondered if he should offer to pay the woman outright. Eastern women were touchy about money, but even he wasn't so sure about paying a woman to marry him. Of course, he'd see that she had plenty of money for her trouble; he'd panned a modest amount of gold in the Black Hills southeast of here this past spring so he had enough. But it just didn't seem right somehow to bring up money quite yet.

Chapter Three

There was a cluster of cottonwood trees leading into the small town of Miles City. The trees were slender and not rooted very deep in the gray alkali soil, but they gave some relief from the vast emptiness that seemed to echo back and forth in this part of the territories. Elizabeth hadn't been prepared for all of this vastness. It felt as though God could look right down and see her, not because He was searching her out, but just because there was so little else in sight. Well, if He wanted to look, she couldn't stop Him. It did make her nervous, though.

She sat on the wagon seat next to Jake. It had rained some on the way here and the dampness had turned the ground dark. It wasn't wet enough to slow down the wagon wheels, though, so Elizabeth had been holding the baby in her arms to protect the little one from the worst of the jostling as they bumped along the rough road. She looked down and smiled.

Elizabeth might not want God looking at her, but she

was glad He knew about the baby. She adjusted the blanket covering the infant and, when she looked up again, Jake had turned the oxen team slightly to enter the town and she could see the main street for the first time.

The trip to Miles City had been slow. Jake had his horse tied to the back of the wagon, and Spotted Fawn had ridden her pony as far away from the wagon as she could while still riding with them.

"Why, it's full of people." Elizabeth couldn't believe it. There were people everywhere and dozens of wagon wheels had made tracks down the street. Her first feeling was relief that she and Matthew hadn't come through this town before he got the fever.

Matthew had everything so well planned. He'd told her it would be okay if he started his store by selling things from the back of their wagon. He figured most of the buildings would be thrown together with bits of canvas and mud-chinked logs so people would not expect to shop in a regular mercantile as they would if they were back East.

But Matthew had been wrong. There were no canvas and rough-hewn huts to be seen. The frame buildings were neatly painted and laid out on two sides of something called Richmond Square. There was even a sign naming the place. That meant someone had money. Miles City was not like the gold-mining towns Matthew had heard about that were thrown together haphazardly because everyone was looking for gold. The gnarled branches of the cottonwoods weren't the kind of trees used to make the plank boards in these buildings.

"Somebody hauled in a lot of lumber." Elizabeth wondered if maybe the town had been rough earlier, but had grown up without Matthew hearing about it.

Jake nodded. "It came in on the steamboats. I brought some of the lumber down from Fort Benton myself. I was going to add onto my place, but I gave it to the school instead."

Elizabeth was glad no one could see the flannel union suits and unbleached muslin Matthew had packed so hopefully in the bottom of their wagon.

"We couldn't afford to take a steamboat," she said. "Not with all the goods Matthew wanted to bring. That's why he got us our wagon. Fortunately, we found a few other wagons still going this way, so we came together."

Elizabeth wondered what she would do with all of the things Matthew had packed in that wagon. Most of it was rough fabrics with little value. The best cloth they had was the red calico cotton she'd dyed herself. It was one of the few things in the bottom of the wagon that truly belonged to her.

Most people wouldn't even have attempted what she'd done, but an old woman had told Elizabeth about the dye process and she'd decided to try it. She liked the name of it—Turkey red oil-boiled dye. It had all sounded so grand and exotic.

She'd been pregnant at the time and wanted some bright red yarn so she could knit a blanket for their baby's first Christmas. Matthew had said it was foolish to give a present to a baby, but she didn't think so. Most of the reds that were dyed in other ways would fade or bleed with each washing and she wanted a blanket that would hold its color for generations to come. She had pictured her baby showing the blanket to his or her own baby in the distant future and telling the little one that Grandma had made the red blanket for a very special Christmas years ago.

A lone rider passed their wagon and Elizabeth was jolted out of her memories. She'd gotten so caught up in thinking about the Christmas yarn that she'd forgotten that her whole reason for making it was now gone. She had no family. No husband to worry about pleasing. She had no use for a red blanket that held its color for generations.

Her life had changed once again and an unbleached gray was enough to mark her endless days. She was sure she could sell the red yarn, and the fabric she'd dyed, too, but she doubted there would be much of a market for the other things she and Matthew had brought west. The people walking in and out of the stores here were not wearing poor clothes. It was mostly men walking around, but there were women, too. And they were clearly used to getting good fabrics.

Matthew hadn't had the money to buy any but the lowest quality. He thought that, by the time people demanded better goods, he would have the money to buy them. His heart would have been broken if he had lived to see his dream fall apart.

Nothing was turning out the way they had planned, Elizabeth told herself as she looked away from the busy street and back at the man sitting beside her on the wagon seat.

She couldn't believe she was going to marry this man. She still felt married to Matthew.

She, Jake and the girls had left the fort before midday. She had put everything back in the wagon and Jake had managed to convince Mr. Miller to return the oxen that were now pulling it. The blacksmith had even thrown in a bag of oats for good wishes on their life together. Elizabeth hadn't known what to say when the man carried out the oats so she'd unpacked six jars of her best canned green beans and given them to him in appreciation.

Jake grunted as he turned and motioned for Spotted Fawn to come closer.

Then he turned to Elizabeth. "This town gets busier every day. Someone put up that hotel hoping that the railroad will stop here. All of the surveying the army is doing has people on edge wondering what route the railroad will take when it comes this way. I tell people it's years away, but no one knows for sure."

Elizabeth thought Jake wanted to say more about the railroad, but he didn't do it so she kept looking around. She noticed that the hotel was only one of several two-story buildings on the street. The rain had turned the top of the ground into a thick mud. Several horses and a buggy were making their way through the street. The wheels didn't sink in far, but the boots of the men walking seemed to pick up a layer of mud.

"Maybe Matthew could have gotten a job clerking in one of these places," Elizabeth said looking down the length of the street. In her heart, though, she knew he would have refused to work for someone else. He would have given up. They would have been even poorer here than they had been back in Kansas. She would have had to take in laundry again and there would have been no one to watch the baby while she lifted the tubs of scalding water.

The laundry itself would have been difficult, too. No one seemed to be wearing simple clothes. The woman hurrying across the street in front of them was holding up skirts that showed lace-trimmed petticoats. Ruffles like that required a hot iron at the end of it all. And the skirt over the petticoats looked as if it was made of blue French serge. It would take extra brushing to keep the double weave looking nice. And no one wanted to pay extra for any of it.

A modest blue hat sat atop the woman's brilliant copper hair. Elizabeth looked at the hair closely. The hair was so colorful she wondered, at first, if it had been dyed with henna. But surely the woman could not get those tones with the dye, so the hair must be natural. Elizabeth almost envied her until the woman lifted her head and finally saw Elizabeth and Jake. The woman glanced up with a vague smile, but as she looked fully at Jake, her expression turned to shock and then to an indignant frown. Elizabeth wondered if the woman was angry with them for some reason, but she hurried off before Elizabeth could ask Jake about her.

"I'll send a note down to the reverend while we buy a few things at the store," Jake said as he slowed the wagon.

Elizabeth forced her attention back to the man beside

her. "Oh, you don't need to do that—buy anything, I mean. Not for me."

"You'll still need things for the girls. Dresses and all."

Elizabeth wondered if Jake knew how much things like that cost. A man who wore buckskin wasn't likely to know how dear fabric was. If it was gingham or calico, the price might not be too bad. But a twill silk or French serge material was impossible. Still, it was nice of him to think of what they needed. It was more than Matthew had ever done. "I know how to get by. We won't need much that's store-bought."

"I want the girls to look like ladies."

"Surely they won't need to—" Elizabeth stumbled when she saw she was giving offense. "Not because they're Indian girls. That's not what I meant."

"They have white blood in them, too. Red Tail was half-white."

"Of course. It's just that they're only girls."

"I want them to have the best dresses possible. We'll order from San Francisco if we have to."

Elizabeth nodded. Now she'd gotten his pride involved. He was probably going to spend money on dresses that they should be saving for winter food. But she knew men well enough to know that she'd only make matters worse by continuing to press him on it. She would sew the dresses herself, of course, and she'd only pick out the cheaper fabrics. Maybe she could even use some of the muslin they had in the wagon. The bark of an oak tree made a light yellow dye that would set the muslin well and the girls wouldn't even notice the material wasn't store-bought.

"You should get a new dress, too," Jake added. "Maybe something in a deep moss green to match your eyes."

She didn't have any dyes that went to a deep green. She had the leavings of some indigo that she could mix with wood ash to make black, but she'd have to buy bolted material to have any kind of a green. "I'd rather have some tea. And maybe a lid to cover my pan so I can steep it properly. "

Tea was cheaper and more to her liking than color-pressed fabric anyway. She'd had the luxury of real tea for a week or so now. A tin of it had been left on the seat of her wagon one morning with the hardtack. She hadn't been able to brew it properly because she only had an open pan to hold it, but she'd enjoyed it immensely. Her conviction that she was dying had made her reckless and she'd used more of the tea than she had intended so she didn't have much left.

Elizabeth felt Jake pull the wagon to a complete halt in front of a building with a large sign that read The Broadwater, Bubbel and Company Mercantile. The store was fronted by a small section of wooden walkway and she could look right into the windows. She had never seen so much merchandise, not even in any of the stores she'd gone to back in Kansas. She was glad she was still wearing her gray silk dress even though she didn't have a proper hat to wear with it.

Jake jumped off the wagon and walked around to take the baby. He slipped the baby into his fur sling before reaching up with the other arm to offer Elizabeth help in stepping down from the wagon. Elizabeth was grateful for the assistance, more to impress anyone who might be watching them than because she needed the help. If they were going to do business in this town, Elizabeth wanted them to look respectable.

The warm smell of spices greeted Elizabeth when she walked through the door that Jake had opened for her. This time Elizabeth didn't want to take any chances on unintentionally offending someone. She smiled at the woman behind the counter. She did not get a smile back. Spotted Fawn had not come in with them so Elizabeth wondered if it was the Indian baby that was causing the upset look in the woman's eyes.

But that couldn't be right, Elizabeth told herself. The furs covered the little one so completely that no one could even tell a baby rested in Jake's arms. The woman was definitely staring at the furs, though. She must have been watching them through the windows.

"Good afternoon, Annabelle," Jake said.

The woman did not answer. Her skin was flushed and her chin defiant. Her face looked kind, even if her eyes were braced for battle and focused on a spot to the right of the doorway. She was past middle-aged and some gray showed in the light brown hair she wore pulled back into a bun. Her white blouse was freshly pressed and her black wool skirt was proper.

Elizabeth thought the other woman wasn't going to answer Jake, but finally she did.

"Good afternoon to you, as well."

Only then did the woman meet Elizabeth's eyes.

Elizabeth forced herself to smile. Even if the woman

wouldn't want to socialize with them for some reason, surely she would be polite. And, if Elizabeth were even more polite in return, the woman would need to continue answering back.

"You have a good store here. Your shelves are completely full. I see coffee and spices. Flour, too," Elizabeth said. "You must be proud."

The store looked well enough stocked to meet anyone's needs. The front counters, showcase and shelves were a dark wood made shiny from repeated rubdowns. To the left, there was a tobacco cutter. Behind the woman there were tins of face powder and hand mirrors with matching brushes. A cracker barrel stood in front of the case. A few leather-bound books lay on the top of the counter.

Farther back, Elizabeth saw a tin of tea that was the same kind that had been left at her wagon. Beside it was a china teapot with lovely pink roses painted on its side.

"It's not my store. I just clerk here," the woman said stiffly.

"Still, you must make recommendations and I can't think of anything your shelves are lacking."

"We do have a good selection," the woman admitted. By now her face looked pale as though she needed to force herself to stand by her words. "For our better customers."

Elizabeth could see Jake's jaw clench.

"I didn't know you had different kinds of customers," Jake said.

Annabelle was silent for a minute. "Your friends were here this morning, after you left."

"Higgins and Wells?"

Annabelle looked miserable, but determined. "Our other customers complained."

"I know they can be a little loud," Jake said. "But I've never known them to mean anyone harm."

The store clerk's face tightened.

"I…ah—" Elizabeth tried to think of something to say to relieve the tension "—I am surprised to see such a fine store. Back in Kansas, we hadn't expected to see something like this way out here. My husband would have—"

Elizabeth faltered to a stop, but then continued. "My husband wanted to own a store like this someday."

Annabelle took her eyes off Jake and turned them toward Elizabeth. Something flickered in the woman's eyes, but she didn't say anything.

Jake looked at the shelves behind the counter and then turned to the clerk. "We need to buy a wedding ring."

Oh, dear, Elizabeth thought. She was not sure she could marry another man who wanted to spend money so freely. She accepted that she would be the one responsible for providing most of the food and clothing. She had always had to do for herself and those around her. But cash money was hard to come by and she didn't like to see it slip away no matter who had worked for it.

"I don't need a new ring," Elizabeth whispered as she leaned closer to Jake. She had no desire to embarrass him in front of the store clerk, but they needed to come to some understanding. "We can use the one I already have."

"I won't use your husband's ring."

Elizabeth watched as the clerk turned to look for

something on the shelf behind the counter. Elizabeth figured the woman was giving them some privacy. She smoothed down the skirt of her dress.

"The ring was my mother's," Elizabeth murmured quietly. She'd been given it at her parents' funeral and had kept it all the years since. Matthew had been relieved that he didn't need to buy a ring for her. "And it's an expense that we don't need."

Elizabeth watched Annabelle turn around and set a tray on the counter. The woman's face softened slightly as she studied Elizabeth. "You're that woman, aren't you? The one out by the fort who lost her husband and baby?"

Elizabeth gave a jerky nod. So that was the problem. "The doctor says I'm past the time of getting the fever, though. You don't need to worry."

The woman reached over and set her hand on Elizabeth's arm. "I felt so sorry for you. I sent a tin of tea out with one of the soldiers. I hope you got it. Tea always soothes me when I don't feel good."

Elizabeth relaxed. Maybe the woman was just cautious with strangers. Or maybe Jake's friends had upset other customers by cursing or something. It was likely a misunderstanding of sorts. Annabelle seemed to be a nice person.

"That tea was such a lovely gift," Elizabeth said as she smiled at the other woman. "I don't know when I've had tea that I've enjoyed as much. I had some sassafras bark in the wagon with me, but I used most of it up when my husband was sick."

Elizabeth didn't think she'd ever be able to drink

sassafras tea again without picturing Matthew dying. Even the smell of it made her feel ill.

The woman nodded. "That tea was from England. We got it with our last shipment."

Elizabeth thought the woman was going to say something more, but instead she glanced up at Jake and all of the friendliness in her face drained away. She looked worried and afraid.

Jake didn't see it because he was looking down at the rings, but Elizabeth did.

"We'll want a gold ring, of course." Jake was looking at the tray of rings the woman had set on the counter. Dozens of rings were lined up in shiny rows.

Annabelle bit her lip and, when she didn't move, Jake looked up.

"Perhaps you would care to wait outside while she tries on the rings," Annabelle suggested softly.

Elizabeth could see the woman had needed to brace herself to say those words.

"Some women like to try on several," Annabelle added as her face flushed.

Jake nodded, although he looked doubtful. "I guess I should see about sending that note to the reverend anyway. Otherwise he'll probably leave the schoolhouse before we get there."

The store clerk watched Jake walk out of the store and close the door before she turned to Elizabeth.

"I can't let you do this," the woman whispered in a rush. She had bright spots of color on her cheeks. "I'm a widow, too. I know what it's like. And he is a striking man. But, surely you're not so desperate that you'll marry him."

Elizabeth stiffened. "I know it's unusual. And I haven't known him long, but he seems like a good, God-fearing man."

Elizabeth saw no need to tell Annabelle about the arrangement she and Jake had made.

Annabelle pursed her lips. "A man like him needs to fear God a little more if you ask me."

A man like what? Elizabeth wondered. "If it's the girls. I know they are Indians, but I understand that Mr. Hargrove is not. Besides, I believe we are all God's creatures."

Elizabeth knew that was stretching the truth. She wasn't sure what she thought about God and the Indians. But she wasn't going to admit that to a stranger in this town where the girls needed acceptance. She owed them that much loyalty at least.

"It's not the girls. It's him."

"Oh." Elizabeth felt herself go cold. "What do you mean?"

"I mean he's a *wolfer*." Annabelle's lips deepened in a disapproving line. "At least those friends of his are. They were in today and, well, it's no conversation for a lady. It's disgusting what they do. Even the Indians are better."

Elizabeth swallowed. "He mentioned that he had done some prospecting for gold and some trapping."

The woman nodded grimly. "The trapping days have been over for years. Even the buffalo are thinning out. What trappers that are left have turned to wolfing. His friends wanted to put in an order for that poison—strychnine—this morning. A big bag of it. I told them no. As though we'd carry that. They kill a buffalo and sprinkle the dead animal with it."

"Oh, dear, you're sure?"

The woman nodded. "I used to think that the one, Higgins, was a good God-fearing man. A little rough in his manners maybe, but he told me he prays and—he even asked if he could walk me home from church if he came someday. I said yes, but then—"

The woman crossed her arms. "Then he started bragging about how he can poison up to sixty wolves in one night the way they do it. And no holes in the pelts, either, so they get top dollar on the furs. All they do is go out and pick up the dead wolves the next morning. With unblemished pelts just like the folks back East want them."

Annabelle paused and looked a little sad. "He's got all the money he needs now, of course. But…to die of strychnine poisoning. Even for a wolf, well, I simply can't condone it. The convulsions. The foaming at the mouth. Besides, other animals die, too—it's not just the wolves. And, birds. I love birds, even the vultures. It's not fair to the animals, they don't have a chance."

"Oh, dear." Elizabeth couldn't believe it. She hadn't known Jake for long, but he didn't seem like a cruel man. She had a bit of poison in her wagon, of course. All dyers did. The indigo leavings used to make a strong black dye were poisonous. She was careful with it, though, and always kept it in a lidded jar so no animal could mistakenly eat it.

"Jake lives out there on Dry Creek by those friends of his. I talked to the manager and he agrees with me. I'm not going to sell the men poison. Decent folks are trying to make Miles City a good place to live. There's talk all the time that someday the railroad representatives will come to town and look us over. I don't want to be selling strychnine to wolfers when that happens."

"So it's not the girls?"

The woman shook her head and then gave a small smile. "Folks around here might shoot an Indian, but they'd spit on a wolfer. If they had the nerve, that is."

"Oh."

"I'm just giving you a word of caution."

"I'm grateful."

Elizabeth realized she was in trouble. She wanted to help the baby, but she didn't see how she could marry someone like Jake. Even if the marriage wasn't real, she would be out there alone with him and the girls—and his wolfer friends. What if they put poison in her tea some morning? She had been willing to die, but she didn't want to be murdered.

"I don't suppose there's any jobs available in town."

The woman frowned. "Virginia Parker got a job recently working at the saloon down the street, playing piano."

"Oh, I couldn't work in a saloon. What decent woman could?"

"I'll not hear anything said about Virginia. She's a fine young woman. There's just not much work around here and most of it's in the saloons."

"Surely there are other jobs. I could teach a little school. Not Latin or anything fancy. But I'm good with numbers."

"The Reverend Olson already teaches school. He even knows Latin. But, between that and his preaching, he barely makes enough to keep body and soul together for him and his wife. The town hasn't exactly gotten around to paying anyone for the school yet. The parents are going to meet to see what they can do about it. My son, Thomas, goes to the school."

"I wouldn't need to make much. It's only me to support."

"Could you sew enough to be a dressmaker?"

"If the styles were simple."

The woman shook her head. "You'd need ruffles and hoops to please this crowd. Most of the regular women make their own dresses. It's the women in the saloons— not Virginia, of course, but the other women—they are the ones willing to pay someone to make dresses for them. But they want French lace and that new kind of shimmering braid they've been asking for. In silver and gold both, mind you. We stock some of the best silks in the world just for them. But, what's a good fabric if the thing doesn't fit right? A handy seamstress could make a good living if she knew fashion."

"I could learn. I'd just need to buy some patterns."

"We don't have any of the new styles yet. The owner hasn't even sent off for them. We have some old ones, of course, but—"

"Oh, well. I suppose I could take in laundry for a while." Elizabeth squared her shoulders. She'd do that if she had to and keep the Indian baby with her for the winter. "I'm used to washing men's shirts and woolens."

The woman shook her head. "Sam Lee does that. You may have seen the sign on your way into town—Good Washing and Fireworks Here? He's a Chinaman who does the laundry for most of the town. He'd be hard to beat."

Elizabeth heard the door to the mercantile open.

"Who'd be hard to beat?" Jake asked as he walked inside and up to the counter. He had the baby in the sling next to his chest. He didn't know what had Annabelle in such a contrary mood, but she couldn't have picked a worse time. He'd come to know her because she went to church most Sundays just as he did. He'd always thought her to be a sensible woman and Higgins had praised her extravagantly the last time Jake had shared their evening fire.

Maybe that was the problem.

"I don't suppose it's Higgins?" Jake asked Annabelle directly. Higgins had been a trapper for decades, as Jake's father had been. The man was said to have wrestled a grizzly once and gone back to chopping wood afterward as if like there had been nothing to it. But for all of the man's courage, he had even less of an idea about how to act around refined women than Jake did.

"I was speaking of the man who does the laundry," the store clerk said stiffly. "Mr. Higgins is none of my concern."

"All right then," Jake said slowly. That should be good, he thought. He turned to Elizabeth. "Did you find a ring that fit?"

"Not quite." Elizabeth hesitated. "Maybe we could use my mother's ring until we find exactly what we want."

Jake searched Elizabeth's face. "If you're sure. Most women like new things."

Something was wrong. Annabelle had stared at his shoulder most of the time she was talking to him and Elizabeth could barely look him in the eye. He supposed she was finally realizing what she was about to do. Not that he could blame her. He knew he had no business marrying someone like her and dragging her into the problems he'd probably have with the people of this town.

Of course, why would that make Annabelle so unfriendly? Maybe it did have something to do with Higgins instead.

"Higgins didn't propose to you, did he?" Jake suddenly asked. Annabelle had been in town for several months now. Her husband had been a miner over by Helena until he'd been shot and killed. But maybe she'd lived back East before that. "I know things are different out here. Most men don't feel they have the time to spend courting, so they just get to the point. But they don't mean any harm by it."

Jake figured he was speaking for himself as well as his friend.

"Mr. Higgins most certainly did not propose," Annabelle protested. Her face had gone a bright pink and she looked indignant. "He knows better than that. He's never even come calling. I'm a widow in mourning. A decent women wouldn't—" Annabelle stopped and looked at Elizabeth. "Oh. I didn't mean—"

Elizabeth waved the words away. "Don't worry about it."

Jake didn't know what had happened to his Elizabeth. All of her indignation was gone. She looked tired. For the first time, he felt the urge to put his arm around her shoulders. He didn't deserve this woman, but he did plan to protect her with all of his might. The problem was he wasn't exactly sure how to protect her from the discouragement Annabelle was causing her.

"You won't need to see Higgins if you don't want to," Jake said quietly to Elizabeth. "I usually just go over and sit with him and Wells at their place anyway."

It was probably best if he kept his old trapper friends away from her.

He could see Elizabeth straighten her shoulders. "Your friends will always be welcome at your home. I wouldn't stand in their way. It's your house."

"It will be your house, too."

Now that they were talking about it, Jake wondered what Elizabeth would think of his house. They were mentioning it as though it was a grand place, but it wasn't. It wasn't even really a house. He supposed it would be considered a cabin if a man were generous in his judging. Jake had given all the smooth lumber he had to the school when they were building that. He was due to get lumber in return when the school had some money, but he planned to let the debt pass. The children needed books more than he needed a better cabin, especially since it was just him.

Jake stopped himself. Of course, he wasn't alone

anymore. He had his nieces and now this woman. The next thing, he'd be getting a dog. He should have built a better place. But, it was too late now. The smooth lumber was gone and his cabin already built.

He had used the logs from some of the cottonwood trees that trailed along the Dry Creek when he built his place. The logs weren't big enough to make a full cabin like they made back East. Folks here dug a trench and put the logs in it upright and then chinked it all together with mud, lime and twigs. They'd done that at the fort. Still, he'd put in a window of real glass opposite the fireplace when he could have just stretched a greased deerskin over the opening. He hadn't bothered with a proper floor, though. Instead, he'd packed the earth down and spread some buffalo hides around.

What had looked to him like a snug home for wintering would not appeal to a woman who'd known better. He was a fool if he thought otherwise. Maybe Annabelle had heard about the house from Higgins and warned Elizabeth about it. Something was upsetting the woman he was planning to marry.

This time Jake did put his arm around Elizabeth's shoulder. Her muscles were tight. He couldn't tell if it was because she was forcing herself to stand there without pulling away or because she was trying not to give in to his embrace. Neither thought comforted him much.

"I don't need your house. I still have my wagon," Elizabeth said as she pulled away slightly and then turned around to start walking out of the store. "Thank you for your help, Annabelle. I appreciate it."

The other woman nodded. "Stop by any time and God's best to you."

Well, if that didn't beat everything, Jake thought. If he'd heard right, his bride was still thinking about wintering in that wagon of hers instead of in his cabin. That didn't make any sense at all, not even for an Eastern woman who didn't know these parts. He still had some things to buy before he left the store. Maybe if he gave her some time alone, the woman he was going to marry would tell him what was wrong.

Elizabeth wondered what she was going to do. She opened the door and took another good look at the streets of Miles City. There were no Help Wanted signs in any of the windows. Maybe the preacher would have some words of advice.

Elizabeth was glad Jake had stayed in the store after she went out on the street. She needed to think. There was a bit of a breeze outside, but Elizabeth scarcely noticed it. The woman with the red hair and blue serge skirt was standing in front of a store on the other side of the street. She had her head bent and was furiously talking to two other women who were both wearing simple calico dresses with sunbonnets. It was good to know there were some plain people in this town. The other women's faces were weathered and pinched.

Whatever the women were upset about, Elizabeth figured it was not as bad as the predicament she was facing. It took a moment for Elizabeth to realize the women across the street had stopped talking and were staring at her. No, it wasn't her. She looked to her left and saw Spotted Fawn.

Jake's niece hadn't moved an inch since Elizabeth first went into the store. Not unless it had been to push farther back into the shadows of the overhang that covered the boardwalk in front of the mercantile. Spotted Fawn might be very still, but she could hardly miss the antagonistic looks those women were sending her.

Elizabeth stepped over to stand beside the girl. "Don't pay them any attention. They're just curious."

Spotted Fawn shrugged. "It does not matter."

Elizabeth recognized that tone of voice. She had said the same kind of words when she was made to feel awkward in her place as the unpaid servant of the houses where she worked back in Kansas. One needed to feel some power in a situation to protest. Without that, a person merely endured.

Just then, Jake came out of the store and started to usher Elizabeth and his niece down the street. He told them they were headed to the schoolhouse.

Elizabeth didn't say anything to Jake about the women. She told herself that they might have been just curious. And they could have been staring at her more than Spotted Fawn anyway. It wasn't often that a woman who was supposed to be dead came to town to go shopping. Maybe one of them had seen her outside the fort and was worried about the fever. That made sense.

They came to a saloon and Elizabeth happened to glance into the half-draped window. She saw a woman standing beside a piano. Her blond hair was swept up and she was wearing a fresh white blouse and a gray skirt. "That woman works there?"

"Only because Colter is a soft touch. Virginia's brother was one of the soldiers killed a few weeks ago so she needs the work. Her other brother is off somewhere prospecting for gold."

"She's not dressed like I would expect."

Elizabeth wasn't sure, but maybe she could work in this saloon if she were allowed to dress like a decent woman and stay in the back of the place. A couple of used glasses were sitting on the counter as the bartender poured whiskey for some man. "Do they pay someone to wash dishes?"

"Usually there's a kid, Danny, who does that, but he's been in jail for a few days. He stole a man's watch," Jake said as he turned to look at her. "But Colter wouldn't hire you, if that's what you're thinking. A lady doesn't belong in a place like that, especially not washing dishes."

"I'm not a lady. Besides, there's nothing to be ashamed of in washing dishes," she continued. "People are entitled to a clean glass no matter what they're drinking."

Jake was looking at her skeptically. "I'd say a woman is entitled to a wedding ring, too."

Elizabeth didn't have anything to say to that. She didn't want a new wedding ring. She didn't want a new husband. But, she had to admit, she did want to spend more of her days holding a baby. And she wouldn't mind seeing a smile on Spotted Fawn's face. She wasn't sure what she'd say when the minister asked if she'd take Jake as her husband.

"What do you do for a living?" Elizabeth suddenly asked as she looked up at Jake.

She saw his jaw tighten.

"I'm not a banker, if that's what you're asking," he said. "I don't rightly know what I am. I panned some gold in the Black Hills, though, and I've got enough to stake myself to some cattle when the time is right. This country is changing and I figure that's the next thing for a man to do."

"You don't poison wolves?"

Jake shook his head firmly. "I don't poison anything."

Elizabeth let out the breath she was holding. Well, that was that. Not that he might not have some other dark secret he was hiding, given the friends that he had.

Elizabeth wondered if there would be any witnesses to the marriage if it did take place. She didn't know anyone she could ask to do it. Those women she'd seen staring at them earlier might be following to see what they were doing, but she couldn't ask them. She even refused to look behind her to see if they were following her and Jake.

Elizabeth reached up to pat her hair. She'd washed herself as best as she could in her tent before folding up the canvas and storing it on top of the wagon earlier. She was glad now that she was clean even if she was rumpled. She might not be good enough to go calling on people, but she was wearing her gray dress. It had been suitable in Kansas; it should be good enough for the streets out here.

Those women could stare at her if they wanted, but

she dared them to find genuine fault. Her dress was so neatly mended that no one could tell where the spark had settled on the skirt or the seam had parted under the arm. And her hair might be slightly damp from the rain, but it was firmly anchored behind her head in a bun.

Footsteps made their own sound in the mud, but Elizabeth didn't pay any attention to them until she heard someone muttering behind her. She looked back and saw the women she'd seen earlier marching straight toward her.

The women did not wait until they were even with Jake before they started talking.

"Where did you get her?" the woman in the blue skirt demanded of Jake.

Elizabeth was taken aback by the hostility in the woman's voice. They must think she was still carrying the fever. Surely it must be fear that brought out such antagonism. Then she felt Jake tense up beside her. The woman was not looking at Elizabeth; she was looking at Spotted Fawn.

"Good morning, Mrs. Barker," Jake said. "This is my niece."

"She's just a child," Elizabeth added. *Who could be afraid of a child?*

"She's a heathen," Mrs. Barker said as though that settled everything. "She needs to be sent back to her people."

"I am her people," Jake said.

"Nonsense. Anyone can look at her and see she doesn't belong with you. You might have lived with some of those people, but that doesn't make you one of them. Take the girl back to her own kind. She belongs with the other heathens out there." Mrs. Barker vaguely waved her hand to the vast unsettled land outside of town.

"She's not a heathen. She believes in the same God that you and I do," Jake said.

"I doubt that very much. You listen to me and you listen good, Jake Hargrove. This town is no place for her kind. God doesn't want people mixing. Everyone should keep to their own kind. That especially goes for the heathens."

"It doesn't say that in the Bible."

"Well, then, it should. We won't stand for it. Mark my words on that."

The women gathered up their skirts and stomped past them, their skirts all swaying as they went.

Elizabeth watched them walk down the street.

"Sorry about that," Jake muttered.

"It's not your fault."

Elizabeth was angry. Even the women who had looked down their noses at her back in Kansas hadn't been this rude. No one should treat anyone as Mrs. Barker and her friends were doing. Before her recent tragedy, Elizabeth would have shrugged off their behavior. But not anymore. She might be all alone in life once again, but she wasn't going to let those women treat an innocent young girl as if she was a criminal just because they didn't like the color of her skin.

Elizabeth knew enough about dyes to know that a piece of cloth could turn out red or yellow or blue and still be the same fabric, woven on the same loom.

Dyeing was just something the maker of a garment did. It didn't make the cloth itself better or worse.

Besides, Spotted Fawn might be an Indian, but she had a family. She had her uncle, Jake. They shared the same blood. He was her people. Elizabeth didn't want to see anything happen to this new family, not if she could help it.

Standing right there, Elizabeth made her decision. She was going to get married. Higgins might put poison in her tea and those women might drive them all out of town, but she'd stand up for Spotted Fawn and the baby until that day. If anyone knew what it was to be all alone at Spotted Fawn's age, Elizabeth did.

"Don't pay them any attention," Elizabeth said in a furious whisper to Spotted Fawn. The girl didn't look as though she'd heard Elizabeth any more than she'd heard the women speaking earlier. If Elizabeth didn't know Spotted Fawn spoke good English, she would have thought the girl hadn't understood what had been said.

They didn't stop walking until Jake brought them to the steps of a white frame building. More humble than the stores and with no walkway out front, the building did have a landing at the top of the steps large enough for a dozen people to stand. They climbed the steps, Jake knocked and a man's voice told them to come inside.

"School is out for the day. The reverend will be expecting us," Jake said as he opened the door.

Spotted Fawn stood to the right of the doorway just as she'd stood beside the door of the mercantile. Elizabeth finally realized the girl didn't feel welcome.

"I hope you'll come inside with us," Elizabeth said to her.

Spotted Fawn made no move.

"You can hold the baby," Elizabeth added softly. "I don't know if there's any place to lay her down inside. Wait a few minutes and come when Jake comes, please."

Spotted Fawn nodded. "I will come."

"Thank you," Elizabeth said as she turned.

She looked back at Jake. "You said I could have some time with the pastor before—"

Jake nodded.

Elizabeth hoped the pastor had some comfort to give to her. It wasn't right to marry another husband when she hadn't made her peace about losing her first one. Granted, it wasn't a real marriage that Jake was offering. And she'd already decided to do it, even if she had a feeling it would cause more trouble for everyone than they would know what to do with. But, still, she'd like to confess what she was doing to a minister. She hoped he understood about the baby.

Chapter Four

The inside of the schoolhouse smelled of damp wool. The children must have played outside and gotten wet before they left this afternoon. Light streamed in the three windows, two located on each side wall and one by the door. There was a glass-fronted wood case beneath one of the side windows and it held plants and leather-bound books. A map was tacked to the wall beside one potbellied stove. Another small stove sat in the opposite corner. Elizabeth could imagine children being very happy here. She took one step into the room as the man in front stood up from his desk.

"You must be Elizabeth," the man said with a welcoming smile. "I'm Reverend Olson. I got Jake's message that you were coming."

The man walked down the aisle between the rough-hewn log benches. Each bench had a long, thin table in front of it. There were inkwells and small pieces of chalk to show the places where students sat. She supposed the children kept their lead pencils with them; they wouldn't want to lose those.

Jake had kept his word and hadn't followed her inside the schoolhouse so Elizabeth had closed the door behind her.

The reverend stopped when he was a few feet away from her. "I only wish I'd been in town when your family had the fever. I was up at Fort Benton picking up some books I'd ordered for the school."

Elizabeth shrugged. "There's nothing you could have done."

She'd guess the man was about fifty years old. His brown wool suit was well-worn, but his white shirt was crisply ironed. His hair was a thick gray and his eyes looked at her with sympathy.

She didn't want sympathy.

"I could still go with you and pray over the grave if you'd like. If you'd find that comforting."

Elizabeth shook her head. "Maybe later. Jake's going to make a marker. Maybe then it would be good to—" Her voice trailed off. She swallowed, but continued in a whisper. That was all she could manage. "Maybe by then I will be able to do it."

She hadn't realized she'd neglected to give a prayer at the burial. The doctor from the fort had read some scriptures over the grave and he had said a prayer. But Elizabeth had been silent. She hadn't cried, either. Not even after everyone else was gone. She hadn't grieved for the ones she'd lost, she'd merely waited to join them. But now—

The reverend nodded. "It's always hard when someone we love dies."

"They were all I had and God took them away for nothing."

"I know it feels that way."

Elizabeth looked up sharply. "Do you have a wife?"

The reverend nodded.

"Then you don't know how I feel." Her whisper was gone. Anger filled her voice. "I had no family before I married Matthew and now—" she spread her hands "—I was trying to be so good. So careful. But now I'm alone again."

"God is with you," the reverend said.

Elizabeth didn't know what to say.

Reverend Olson smiled encouragingly at her. "I know it's not always easy to see His hand in our lives, but He loves us all the same."

Elizabeth couldn't keep silent. She'd kept the words inside until now, but it all came bubbling out of her. "I don't care if He loves me. I don't love Him anymore. He took my Rose. That's the end—"

Elizabeth stopped. Her cheeks were burning. She'd been right earlier when she had begged God to let her die. If He'd done it when she asked, she never would have spoken this blasphemy aloud. She could have saved them both the accusation in her voice and the pity on the reverend's face. She wondered if she had damned her soul forever.

The reverend put his hand on her shoulder. "He understands how you feel."

Elizabeth just stood there. If God understood her, He understood more than she did. She just wanted time to go backward to those days when her family was alive. Her only consolation had been the hope of being with Rose and Matthew soon in Heaven and God was not even giving her that comfort. He might never give her that blessing now, not when her feelings were out in the open where everyone could see them. How was she going to live without her baby?

Jake stood outside of the schoolhouse door. It had been almost half an hour since Elizabeth had gone inside. Spotted Fawn had wanted to hold the baby and he had given the little one to her. He couldn't hear anything inside the schoolhouse. He wondered if Elizabeth was changing her mind about marrying him.

Well, if she was, he couldn't blame her. It wasn't just the harshness of the land that might deter her. Mrs. Barker had just demonstrated the extra problems any woman would have in this town if she married him. A woman who was used to the ways of the polite world couldn't be faulted for wanting to avoid that.

And Mrs. Barker had been more charitable than she might have been. Jake suspected there were people in this town who would say he belonged with the heathens as much as the girls did. To them, it didn't matter what a man believed; everything turned on the way someone looked and he still looked more like a mountain man than a gentleman.

Jake was questioning whether he should open the

door and tell Elizabeth he understood. He might as well save her the agony of admitting she was going back on her decision. Besides, he had an ominous feeling about Mrs. Barker. He was half-surprised that the woman hadn't followed them to the schoolhouse to complain to the reverend that he and Spotted Fawn were dirtying the steps by standing on them.

Mrs. Barker liked to believe the church could not go forward without her guidance, but she held things back more than drove them forward. And it wasn't just the church that suffered. It was the whole town.

If it weren't for her talk about the railroad, people wouldn't listen to her. In Jake's opinion, the railroad was fool's gold. It might or might not ever come by here. Unfortunately, Mrs. Barker had a cousin who worked for one of the big railroads back East and somehow she'd used that to make herself the local judge of what a railroad wanted in a town they'd consider for a regular stop.

If she and her Civic Improvement League said one of the saloons needed to wash their windows every week, the windows were washed. If they said the hotel needed to get more bathtubs for their guests, the order was sent back East. Everyone wanted Miles City to be a railroad stop and they were willing to obey Mrs. Barker to see that it happened.

Just then the door opened and Reverend Olson asked Jake and Spotted Fawn to come inside. Jake let his nieces go into the schoolhouse and then stepped inside himself, wondering what he would find.

Elizabeth stood at the front of the room. The afternoon sunlight was shining through the window and surrounding her with its glow. She had a small red flower in her hand.

Jake was stunned.

"It's a geranium," Elizabeth said when she saw him looking at it. "The reverend had a plant and he offered me a bloom for my bridal bouquet."

Jake felt suddenly conscious of the dried mud on his boots. And the creases in his shirt. He'd tied his hair back with a string of rawhide, but he smoothed it down anyway. He should be wearing a suit. Not that he owned one, but he should have tried to borrow one from the officers at the fort. Sergeant Rawlings probably had one.

Elizabeth was smiling at him. Not a big smile, granted. But she looked as though she was well enough pleased to be standing where she was.

"I should have gotten you a ring. If you wait a minute, I'll go back and get one." Jake realized with a start that he was as nervous as an untried colt. Until this very minute, part of him had assumed Elizabeth would have the sense to back out of their agreement. He'd even given her a half hour with the reverend. Surely the good man had talked some sense to her.

"Or flowers. Maybe I can find some proper flowers." He could almost see his mother shaking her head over that little geranium blossom.

Elizabeth shook her head. "We don't need to fuss."

Jake didn't agree. Elizabeth looked like a bride. Not just because of the flower, but also because her face was

all pink and glowing. She looked very pleased with herself. And beautiful in that quiet way she had.

"You're okay with all of this?" he asked her. He
needed to give her one last chance to change her mind.

But Elizabeth nodded. "Reverend Olson made me
realize that, if I had died before Rose, she would have
needed another woman to help her live. The fever could
have taken me as easily as it took Matthew. So I'm doing
this for Rose in a way. I consider it an honor to help."

Jake felt her words like a kick to his stomach. He
didn't know what he had been thinking. Of course, this
wasn't about him. He wouldn't be able to please this
woman any more than he'd pleased his mother. Elizabeth wasn't marrying him with any hope in her heart
related to him. She was being a dutiful martyr, giving
herself up to keep a helpless baby alive.

Well, Jake decided, he couldn't complain. That had
been their agreement.

He glanced over to where Spotted Fawn sat on one
of the benches with the baby on her lap. Those two
were all he needed to worry about.

"Ready?" Reverend Olson asked as he walked over
to look out the window. "I see my wife and her sister
coming. They've agreed to be witnesses."

"We decided to do the minimum." Elizabeth looked
up at Jake. "None of the sickness and health—just the
'I dos.'"

"Is that legal? I don't mind promising to take care of
you."

"Well, but it doesn't mean anything, does it? Not

when we're already planning to annul the marriage in the spring."

Jake felt his frown deepen. He turned to the reverend. "Are you okay with that? An annulment?"

"All I ask is that you give God time to work in your hearts," Reverend Olson said as he opened his Bible. "There's the baby to think about, and besides He might surprise you."

Jake felt Elizabeth flinch beside him. Then he heard the door open and the footsteps of the two women as they walked forward.

"Can we begin?" Elizabeth asked.

"Of course," Reverend Olson said as walked to the front of the aisle and looked down at his Bible. He began to read.

Elizabeth tried not to listen. She didn't want to hear about anything but the good thing she was doing for the baby. If she kept remembering that it could be some other woman doing this for her Rose, she felt good. If she thought about getting married, she felt a little, well, panicked.

Elizabeth calmed herself. She knew how to be a servant in someone else's house and that is the way it would be for her in Jake's. The reverend had been right when he pointed out that she needed Jake's provision as much as he needed her help. It was an agreement much like the ones she'd made with those families when she'd been a girl. She knew what to expect with those arrangements; she'd be fine until spring. Living in those households hadn't made her part of a family any more than living in Jake's house would make her his wife.

"It's time," the reverend whispered to her and Elizabeth realized she'd missed the reading of the vows.

"I do," she said. It didn't matter if she had missed everything. She knew what her job would be. Cooking, cleaning and taking care of the baby. Really, it wouldn't be so bad. She'd get to hold the baby whenever she wanted and she wouldn't need to winter in the wagon.

It would be better than washing glasses in some saloon in town. If the truth were told, she wasn't so sure she could have wintered in a saloon, even if she was in the back where she didn't have to see the customers. She wondered how life would be for that woman who was playing the piano in that place.

Elizabeth forced her mind back to the present. She'd just heard Jake make his own vow to take her as his wife.

It was quiet for a moment. Then one of the women standing behind the reverend cleared her throat quietly.

Elizabeth was going to turn to leave but the minister continued.

"You may now kiss the bride," Reverend Olson announced firmly.

Elizabeth looked at the minister in astonishment. He knew it was not that kind of a wedding. But there was no missing the hope on the older man's face. Or on the faces of his wife and sister-in-law. Elizabeth was going to protest, but she already felt Jake's hands on her shoulders.

Oh, my. She looked up and his eyes darkened. Maybe it was the shadows inside the schoolhouse, but he looked as if he meant something by the way his hand was tipping her chin up to meet his lips.

Elizabeth didn't have time for her back to stiffen. She told herself that was why her knees felt a little weak. Jake was thoroughly kissing her. Oh, my. Even Matthew hadn't coaxed her lips apart quite so sweetly or slipped his hand around to the small of her back as though he knew she needed a little support.

Jake had been hit over the head once. He hadn't passed out, but he'd seen a star or two floating around while he caught his breath. He never knew a man could feel the same way after a simple kiss.

He'd have to have a word with the Reverend Olson. The man had meant well, but he had set in motion something Jake did not want to think about. Of course, Jake didn't want to think about much of anything. He'd rather share another kiss with the surprising Elizabeth O'Brian. He wondered if she knew he could feel her melting into his arms.

Jake heard a woman's indignant gasp and he thought it was Elizabeth until he realized she couldn't be gasping and kissing him at the same time. He lifted his head just in time to see the pink rising in Elizabeth's cheeks. He was tempted to leave his gaze there, but he looked higher and saw Mrs. Barker standing in the doorway of the schoolhouse with one arm pointed heavenward like an avenging angel.

"This is outrageous," the woman said. Her hat was halfway off her head, but she didn't hesitate. She bristled as she led her charge into the schoolhouse. Her two friends meekly followed her, looking around, unsure if they should be there.

Mrs. Barker stood at the front of the church and glared at the reverend's wife. "I didn't expect to see you here at this—this—"

"A man's entitled to kiss his wife," Jake interrupted mildly.

"I don't care who you kiss," Mrs. Barker spat out as she put her hands on her hips. She turned her frown to Jake. "But I'll have you remember this is our children's schoolroom."

"I'm sure Jake is well aware of that," Reverend Olson said.

"Just so he knows he doesn't have the right to interfere with the education of our children."

"School's not in session," Reverend Olson said. "This is also the church and, as such, the proper place for two people to be married. My wife and I will have everything back in place and ready for school tomorrow morning in plenty of time for the children. You don't need to worry."

Mrs. Barker walked halfway back down the aisle until she was standing next to the bench where Spotted Fawn sat. "There won't be any children here tomorrow until we get one thing settled."

Jake took a few steps closer to his nieces so he was standing between them and the woman. "We'll settle it later and alone."

Mrs. Barker didn't stop. She leaned around Jake and

pointed at Spotted Fawn. "This school is for the children
of this town. Not for heathens like her."

Elizabeth gasped. "She's not a heathen."

"She is an Indian. And I want it to be clear that she
won't be going to school here. Not with my children or
any other children of Miles City."

Jake grunted. If he were facing a man, he'd know
how to handle him. Mrs. Barker required something
else. It took him a second to think of what it was.
"You're forgetting that I own half the lumber in this
school. Spotted Fawn will go to school here if I say so."

Even Mrs. Barker couldn't argue with that.

"Is that true?" Mrs. Barker turned to the minister.

The Reverend Olson nodded, his satisfaction evident.
"Don't you remember, we thanked him at the dedica-
tion of the building?"

"Well, that doesn't mean he has any say over the
whole school. You'll see. The Civic Improvement
League won't stand for it. Will they?" Mrs. Barker
turned to the two women who had followed her inside
and they shook their heads dutifully.

With that, Mrs. Barker gave a curt nod to the
reverend's wife, turned around and righted the hat on her
head before marching out of the schoolhouse. Her two
friends followed in her wake.

There was a moment of stunned silence after they
were gone.

"She'll calm down," the minister said. "That Civic
Improvement League of hers can't even agree on what
kind of flowers to plant beside the schoolhouse."

"Rosebushes," his wife said. "Virginia Parker needed someplace to transplant them after she left her lodgings at the fort. The council finally voted to accept them."

"Good choice," Jake said.

"They weren't too sure since Virginia plays the piano in that saloon now."

"Virginia Parker is the same woman today as she was when she lived at the fort with her brother," Jake said. "I know for a fact she's not doing anything in that saloon she couldn't do in church. For pity's sake, she spends the afternoon playing hymns and Colter sends her home before it gets dark. Some people in this town are just too close-minded for their own good. Make that everybody's good."

With that, Jake gathered up his new family and wished the reverend and his wife a good day. His home might be humble, but Jake wanted to walk through his own door with his family and shut the rest of the world out.

Miles City was not the place he wanted any of them to be right now.

By the time they were getting close to his cabin, though, Jake wished he hadn't left town in such a hurry. If he had waited for a couple of hours, it would be dusk when they came upon his cabin. He should have taken everyone to dinner in the hotel dining room. Then it would be sundown and the shallow light would hide some of the flaws of his place. Spotted Fawn and the baby had been staying in his house, of course, so they were comfortable there, but he wasn't sure what Elizabeth would think of it.

He'd built the cabin into the side of a ravine close to the creek. The back wall was made with cottonwood logs, but he'd dug out a space in the ravine so that only half of the wall showed aboveground. The Lakota didn't bother him because of Red Tail and the Crow knew him from the times he'd scouted for the army. He hadn't wanted to announce his cabin's presence any more than necessary, though, because the Blackfeet sometimes came through here. A few trees blocked the view of the cabin so no one would see it until they were almost upon the place.

The lean-to was built into the ground next to the cabin, the logs standing upright in a deep ditch he'd dug for them. He kept his horses there and he'd made the place almost as big as the cabin. He was glad he'd done that now that he'd be spending the nights there with the animals. He'd even had the foresight to build a small loft over half of the space so he'd be able to sleep in peace.

Elizabeth had been quiet for most of the trip out of Miles City and Jake suddenly wondered if she was as nervous about seeing his house as he was about showing it to her.

They were almost close enough to see the cabin now.

"It's built tight," he said. "I chinked and daubed the walls myself. And, being close in to the ground like it is, it stays a little warmer in bad weather."

He'd mixed a good amount of lime with the clay mud he'd used in the daubing and taken only the best twigs for his chinking, too. No one could say his place wasn't well built even if it was humble.

"I've read about sod houses," Elizabeth said quietly.

"It's not really sod." Jake was miserable. He was thinking what Mrs. Barker or even Annabelle would think if he offered them up a sod house. Women expected more. "It's mostly logs."

The cabin came into full view just as Jake had known it would. The window was dirty. He should have cleaned it after the last rain, or at least the rain before that. The ground in front of the door was packed down. He'd meant to put some logs in that place to make a sitting porch, but it looked more like a dried mud puddle than anything at the moment.

His horse, tied to the back of the wagon, saw the lean-to and gave an excited snort. He knew they were home.

"I haven't had a chance to do much cleaning," Jake muttered as he took the baby and then helped Elizabeth down from the wagon. Spotted Fawn was wisely staying on her pony and keeping her distance. Jake wished he could let Elizabeth go into the cabin alone, but he wasn't a coward. He had to admit he'd rather face a charging bear than follow her into that house, but he'd do it anyway.

When she stepped inside the door, Elizabeth smelled sage. She'd never known a man who kept herbs. A large stone fireplace stood on the wall to her right. A black cast-iron hook reached out of the fireplace so a pot could be hung for cooking even though there was also a fine-looking cookstove sitting in the corner. Several pots were scattered on shelves next to the fireplace.

A large table stood in the middle of the room. The

legs were made of slender logs with the bark peeled away. The surface was planed lumber, one board lined up next to another so it was smooth. A coal oil lamp stood in the middle of the table with a glass globe that would do justice to a parlor back East. Three straight-backed chairs sat around the table. She thought they were made of oak.

On the far side of the room, Elizabeth saw a bed piled high with blankets and furs. She quickly looked away from that. Midway down the side wall was a rope ladder hooked over a peg in the wall. The ladder led up to a loft area.

The most surprising thing in the room was the rocking chair that sat beside the fireplace. It was a dark wood, she'd guess it was mahogany, and the sides were well-rubbed with some kind of oil so the whole thing had a soft sheen. It was as fine a chair as Elizabeth had seen in the houses where she worked back in Kansas. All it lacked was a back cushion.

"I can bring your things inside," Jake said from the doorway.

Elizabeth turned around to face him. "Thank you. Just the satchel, please. Your place is lovely."

Jake grunted. "There's wood to build a fire."

Jake left the cabin before he could do any more damage. He should have more to say to his new wife than to ask her to build a fire. Maybe he could think of something more pleasant to say when he brought her satchel inside. Something about the color of her eyes or the shine of her hair. Women set great store by compliments.

He usually wasn't so tongue-tied, but nothing had prepared him for a wife who made him nervous. That kiss had been his undoing. There was a sweetness inside Elizabeth that reminded him of all he was missing in life. Maybe, even if she was new to this land, she could come to be content living here. With him.

Chapter Five

Elizabeth couldn't go to sleep even though it was past midnight. The coals from the banked fire cast a dim light around the cabin and everything was quiet. Spotted Fawn was asleep in the loft and the baby was curled up in the rough wooden crib that Jake had fashioned beside the bed.

Everything was peaceful, but Elizabeth was restless.

Maybe it was that she was lying in a bed, she thought to herself. On the way here, she'd spent so many nights stretched out on the ground and then she'd slept on even harder ground outside of the fort. Her body had forgotten how nice it was to have some softness to lie on as she slept.

Besides, it was her wedding night. She smiled in the darkness. The marriage might not be real, but the night seemed momentous nonetheless. She had been pronounced a wife for the second time in her life. She'd felt a little skittish today until she was sure Jake was going to abide by his agreement.

After seeing how fiercely protective he was of his

nieces, she had started to trust him, though. She hoped he had enough furs in his lean-to. He'd said he would be fine out there and she was going to take him at his word. He'd been a real gentleman about giving up the cabin and she appreciated it. If nothing else, she needed some privacy to nurse the baby.

For the first time since she'd agreed to Jake's suggestion that they marry, she thought everything might work out fine. She would stay until spring. She'd spent longer than that working at different homes as a girl. Back then, she'd figured out how to work in the midst of a family and still keep her heart separate. She could do the same now.

This was a good place for her. Not only would she save the baby's life, but she would have some time to decide what to do next. She wondered if, come next spring, she could go to a town smaller than Miles City and open the store she and Matthew had envisioned. Maybe she'd ask Annabelle the next time they were at the store. She might know of a community that would welcome cheaper goods. She might even be able to dye some of their goods to make them more appealing.

Elizabeth had managed to drift off when she heard the first yell.

"Ahhh," she squeaked as she bolted straight up in bed. She wondered if she'd imagined the yell, but then she heard the banging of tin—*was it tin cups?* And then another yell. And some heavy bells. *Were they cowbells?*

Elizabeth stood up and pulled a blanket off the bed to wrap around herself. She'd heard similar sounds not so long ago when the men got paid at the fort. There must be a bunch of drunken soldiers outside. She couldn't begin to guess what they were doing here, but she intended to find out.

Elizabeth was at the door of the cabin when she heard Spotted Fawn climbing down the rope ladder. The girl had slept in her clothes.

"Don't open the door," Spotted Fawn whispered as she reached the floor and then looked around wildly before racing to pick up one of the cast-iron skillets from the shelves.

"It's okay," Elizabeth said as she arranged the blanket around her so that none of her nightclothes showed. "It's just some foolish drunks."

Elizabeth figured the soldiers would be sick as dogs come morning, but she couldn't do anything about that. She'd put a stop to their noise tonight, though. She opened the door and stepped outside.

"Oh." She almost turned to go back inside. The moon was shining and she could make out two hulking men sitting atop two equally massive black horses. The men were waving their arms and banging on things. The horses were rearing up and stomping their feet. It sounded like a fort full of men and there were only the two of them.

Elizabeth heard the door to the lean-to open and saw Jake step outside. If she hadn't been so worried about those strange men, she would have been concerned about Jake catching a night chill. She could feel the frost on her feet. He must be freezing. Jake had taken time to reach for his rifle, but he hadn't bothered to pull on any of his shirts.

"What do you think you're doing?" Jake yelled at the men.

Elizabeth was mesmerized. She forgot all about the fearsome horses and the men who rode them. Jake was beautiful in the moonlight, the muscles in his arms defined and strong as he moved. She was relieved to see he didn't raise the rifle he held in his hands. That must mean he at least knew these men.

"Heard you got yourself married," one of the men called down from his horse. The man was grinning at Jake. "We didn't have a present handy so we thought we'd give you a proper shivaree."

The horses and the men were all facing the lean-to. Elizabeth was going to turn around and go back inside when the other man noticed her.

"Well, this must be the bride right here," the man said as he turned his horse to face her. He tipped his hat. "It's all my pleasure, ma'am. Jake, here, he'll make a good…" The man's voice trailed off in puzzlement as he looked over at Jake and then back at Elizabeth. "Did we get it wrong? We heard the wedding had happened already."

Elizabeth felt a blush crawl up her neck and she pulled the blanket closer to her. The men were wondering why Jake wasn't sleeping in the cabin with her since they were married. Well, she supposed it was a logical question even if it was none of their concern.

"You heard right." Jake's voice was strong and held more than a hint of warning. "Come back another day and I'll introduce you."

"Breakfast," Elizabeth added brightly. She didn't

suppose Jake liked his friends knowing about their arrangement, but it was too late for that. "Why don't you come back for breakfast? I'll make you some raised biscuits."

"With molasses?"

Elizabeth nodded. "All the molasses you want. And jam, too."

"You don't have to ask us twice. We'll be here."

Elizabeth hoped the thought of biscuits would make those two men forget all about the Hargrove sleeping arrangement. She'd fry up some salt pork, too. And maybe soak some of the dried apples she had in the wagon.

"Just let the sun come up first," Jake called after the men as they started to ride off.

Then he turned to Elizabeth. "You didn't need to do that. We could have just sent them away."

Elizabeth shrugged. "They're your friends. They meant well."

Jake walked closer and grinned. "They meant to wake us up is what they meant. And they did a pretty good job of it."

Jake stood there for a minute, just looking down at her.

"You'll catch cold," Elizabeth finally said. The moon had gone behind some clouds, but she could still see Jake like a shadow in the dark night. If it wasn't so fanciful, she almost thought she could feel the heat of him as he stood there.

He gave her a half smile. "I was just thinking that I never did give you the present I bought for you today."

"You bought me a present?" Elizabeth asked in soft astonishment. No one had ever given her a present. Not even on her real wedding day with Matthew. "Oh, you mean the tea."

Jake shook his head. "There's more. Let me get it. I slipped it into the back of the wagon. Go inside and get warm. I'll bring it in."

Elizabeth nodded. This was a most extraordinary day. Someone had bought her a present.

The inside of the cabin was dark, but Elizabeth could feel her way to the table and then to the fireplace. She reached into the box that sat next to the fireplace and pulled out a short log. She gently placed it onto the fire and sparks flew up and then died down as the fire took hold again. Once she had the fire going, she used a small stick to light the coal oil lamp.

When Jake opened the door a few minutes later, the cabin was glowing with light.

Elizabeth smiled up at him. She had smoothed back her hair and pulled an old calico dress over her nightgown. It might look strange, but it was more decent than just sitting there as she was.

Jake was carefully holding a wooden box as he walked into the room. He set the box on the table and then sat down in one of the chairs himself.

"I hope you like it," he said.

"I'm sure I will," Elizabeth said.

She sat down in one of the chairs and Jake slid the box over to her.

The box was open on the top and newspaper was

stuffed in the corners of the box, covering whatever was there.

"Go ahead," Jake urged her.

Elizabeth pushed the paper aside and there it was—the round china teapot with the delicate pink roses that she'd seen in the mercantile earlier. She'd never had a teapot before in all her life. She pulled the pot out of the box. It even had a lid that fit right on top so she could brew her tea properly. She'd never touched anything so fine and it was hers.

Jake figured he had done it now. His bride sat there looking as if she was on the verge of tears. "Don't cry."

"I never cry," Elizabeth whispered and then she cleared her throat. "Never."

"I shouldn't have gotten the one with the roses," he said. "I didn't mean to remind you—I thought you'd like it best."

"It's beautiful."

"You're sure. We can take it back. They had one that was plain."

"I love roses."

Jake smiled. There was no mistaking the sincere gratitude in his bride's eyes. "Oh, well, then—I'm glad you like it."

Elizabeth put the teapot back in the box. "I'll treasure it forever."

She started to replace the paper that had been packed around the pot.

"You are planning to use it, aren't you?" Jake had felt

something inside him relax when he knew she liked his gift. But now he had the feeling that she was going to keep the teapot in a trunk somewhere.

"But I don't want it to break," she protested.

"If it breaks, I'll buy you another one."

Jake watched Elizabeth's face color up in astonishment and then go flat again.

"Yes, of course," she said, the joy gone from her voice. "I'll leave it on the shelf."

"You can make tea in it whenever you like."

Elizabeth nodded. "It is a great addition to the kitchen here."

Jake wished he knew a little more about women. He was beginning to think his mother wasn't the best example to go by. This woman didn't fret about the things that had upset his mother. He'd given Elizabeth a gift and she'd accepted it with pleasure. And then—

"What's wrong?" he asked softly.

She looked up at him and her eyes were stricken.

"I'll need to leave it with you when I leave," she said. "It'll only break on the road and—I don't even know where I'll be and you'll be—"

Jake grinned. "It doesn't matter where you are. Just get me word if the thing breaks and I'll bring you a new one."

"But I could be miles from here."

Jake nodded. "Still, you have my word. I've got a couple of good horses. I'll bring you a new one."

He would do it, too. He liked thinking Elizabeth would call on him someday in the future if she needed something. "You can call on me for anything."

"Well, thank you then. Instead of setting it on the shelf, I might leave it out on the table. That way the girls can enjoy the roses, too, and—" Elizabeth stopped and looked around. "Oh, dear—"

Elizabeth pointed to the window. It was partially opened. "I think Spotted Fawn—

"Spotted Fawn," Elizabeth stood up and called toward the loft. "Spotted Fawn, are you there?"

There was no answer from the loft.

"She must have gone outside," Elizabeth said. "She was frightened by your friends."

Jake stood up, too. "I should have thought of that." He started to walk toward the door. "It must have reminded her of being with the tribe when—" Jake looked at Elizabeth. He didn't want to upset her any more than she was already. "Stay here. I'll find her."

Even though Jake had asked her to stay in the cabin, Elizabeth would have gone to help him look if the baby didn't need someone to stay with her. How had she forgotten about Spotted Fawn? The girl had been so upset, Elizabeth knew she should have checked on her the first thing when she stepped back inside the cabin. That's what a mother would have done.

A mother would have known what was bothering the girl, too. She should have known the terror in the girl's eyes earlier was enough to make her bolt.

Elizabeth had usually worked as a cook. Of course, she'd also done more than her share of laundry and scrubbing floors. But she'd never been in charge of children before. Or small animals, either. For some reason, it had never occurred to her that she'd avoided taking care of anyone or anything that needed mothering—until Rose.

She wondered if that was why God had taken Rose from her. Maybe He knew she wouldn't do it right. Being a mother required constant attention. The worst that would happen if she was inattentive in her cooking was that something would burn. But being a caretaker meant something serious could happen if she was day-dreaming about teapots instead of making sure someone was where they were supposed to be.

Elizabeth knew Jake needed a mother for the girls more than he needed a cook, but she wished she was only in charge of feeding this family. She would have to do better if she hoped to keep up her end of the bargain. She had known the baby would need her help, but she hadn't thought about the girl.

The fire had burned down to embers before Jake brought Spotted Fawn back. He was carrying the girl and, if it wasn't for the shivering, Elizabeth would have thought the girl was asleep in her uncle's arms. Her calico dress was too light for the night air and she wasn't wearing the animal pelts around her legs as she had been earlier in the day.

"I should have seen to it that she had a blanket with her, at least," Elizabeth said. She'd make sure of it next time, somehow. "Here, let me get the fire going better."

Elizabeth stood up and put a small log in the fire before walking over to the bed and pulling some of the covers off of it. "These will help."

Jake took the blankets she handed to him and set himself in the rocking chair, with Spotted Fawn in his arms. He covered the girl. "We'll just sit here for a while until everyone is warm."

Elizabeth sat back down at the table and watched Jake rock his niece. She felt miserable. If she had failed so completely at a task for one of the families who had taken her in when she was Spotted Fawn's age, Elizabeth would be packing her mother's old satchel about now, getting ready to move on to the next family.

But there was no next family here. She'd be here for the winter.

Elizabeth wondered now if she had chosen to spend her time in the kitchens of those various homes so she wouldn't be called upon to take care of the children of the households. Elizabeth knew her heart had been broken when Rose died, but she was beginning to wonder why she hadn't had a lesser heartbreak years ago when she left the children of some household. She couldn't even remember being sad about leaving a kitten behind. She had never let herself be responsible for any living thing. The closest she had come was tending her garden every summer. But then, no one grew overly fond of a carrot or a tomato.

Elizabeth looked over at Spotted Fawn as she cuddled against Jake's shoulder. The girl was gripping Jake's buckskin shirt even in sleep. Whatever was troubling her, it probably didn't have an easy solution.

No child except Rose had ever clung to Elizabeth.

Not that it would be wise to become attached to this

family. They had more problems than she could solve.
Elizabeth reminded herself that she was only here
because the baby needed to nurse. Spotted Fawn resented
her and Jake had been all too willing to say she could
leave in the spring. No, this was not the place to form any
attachment, but when she left here she might just look
for a simple family who had children who needed care.

The floor of the cabin was nothing but hard dirt, but
that suited Elizabeth. She walked back to the bed and
leaned down by the head of the bed so she could draw a
series of lines in the floor. She would mark her days in
this household. Four months should be enough for the
baby. Elizabeth guessed the infant was already a few
months old. It wouldn't be long before it could survive on
soft food like well-cooked potatoes and mashed carrots.

Elizabeth would set aside the canned goods that
could be used for the baby. And, when the time came,
she would start to look for an uncomplicated family
who needed someone for their children.

She glanced back at Jake and his niece. She still
didn't know what had upset Spotted Fawn and it didn't
look as though she'd learn anything tonight. They were
both sitting in the rocking chair, dozing. The blankets
had fallen to the floor. She walked over and picked up
the heaviest blanket, tucking it in around them both.

She hated to say it, but she was bound to this family
for the moment. Until she left, she'd do her best to take
care of them.

Chapter Six

Mr. Wells was sincerely interested in breakfast, Elizabeth decided as she slid a second batch of biscuits onto the tin plate she'd found on the shelf. It turned out most of the bulk she'd seen on him last night had been from his buffalo coat. The man himself was tall and something in the way he moved reminded her of a stalk of wheat, bending this way and that with his head looking down half of the time. She decided the man must be shy. Or just not used to being around women. Or maybe not interested in talking to anyone, period.

Jake's other friend, Mr. Higgins, was definitely not shy. He reminded her of a grizzly, both because of the size of him and the kind gruffness that was evident in his voice as he talked and laughed. He didn't just talk to her, either, for which she was pleased. He also included a few comments to Spotted Fawn, trying to get the girl to smile back at him. For that alone, Elizabeth forgave him for interrupting their sleep last night.

The men were sitting at the table in the middle of the room. Spotted Fawn was in the rocking chair, holding the baby. Elizabeth was moving between the stove and the table.

"The apples are almost ready," Elizabeth said. She had crushed some cinnamon to put on the sauce she'd made of dried apples and walnuts. She'd cooked the soaked apples, but she wanted to be sure the spices didn't overpower the taste of the fruit so she'd waited to add the cinnamon until she pulled the pan off the stove.

She'd gotten up at first light and started the fire so she'd have the stove hot enough to make her biscuits. She'd pulled an apron out of her satchel to cover the old calico dress she had been wearing.

"It sure smells good," Higgins said.

Elizabeth nodded and tried to smooth down her dress with her free hand. She didn't want Jake to be ashamed of his new wife so she had planned to change into her gray dress before the men got here. She'd practically slept in the old calico one and it was wrinkled. But the stove had given her some problems. And she hadn't found any flour so she'd had to go out to the wagon and get some of hers.

And then she had remembered that the men who were coming to breakfast were wolfers. Biscuits and applesauce didn't seem like enough to feed men like that, not even when she added some salt pork to the frying pan. In the end, she'd pulled out a jar of her sour cabbage to use with the salt pork in case the men wanted more than biscuits. This was the first meal she'd made in Jake's house and she wanted him to be proud of her.

"Yes sir, this is a mighty fine meal, ma'am," Higgins said. He lifted his shaggy head and looked at Elizabeth as she set the applesauce on the table. "I don't know when I've tasted anything as good as what you've got right here."

"Thank you," Elizabeth said quietly. She was wondering if she should have forgotten about the sour cabbage and changed her dress. Jake was scowling. Oh, he was sitting at the table as if everything was fine and, when she looked at him square on, his face was pleasant enough. But when she turned, and he couldn't see that she saw him, he was definitely scowling.

It had to be the dress. Matthew had never liked it when she wore old clothes, either. She should have invited the men for dinner instead of breakfast. At least then she would have had all day to prepare the food and make sure she was well-dressed.

Elizabeth lifted her head. Men never did understand the work that was involved in seeing to their comfort.

"It's my pleasure to feed someone like you," Elizabeth said to Higgins. At least someone appreciated the fact that she'd cooked the biscuits and put up jam last summer so they could eat it now. She hadn't worn her silk dress when she'd picked those wild strawberries, either. "You're a real gentleman about it, too, Mr. Higgins."

Mr. Wells gave a snort of amusement.

But Mr. Higgins reared back in astonishment. "Me? You think I could pass for a gentleman?"

"Well, I… Of course." Elizabeth remembered that she was speaking to a wolfer. Still. "A man can be as much of a gentleman as he chooses to be."

* * *

Jake should have known a woman would be trouble. He'd no sooner gotten married than Higgins was eyeing his wife. Oh, the other man probably thought Jake didn't know what was going on, but Higgins hadn't taken his eyes off Elizabeth since he had come in the door this morning.

Of course, Wells hadn't been much better, but it was pretty obvious that when Wells had been looking at Elizabeth and salivating like a lost dog, he was really more interested in the biscuits that she had been holding than the woman herself.

Higgins, though, hadn't eaten enough to feed a grass-hopper. Elizabeth probably wouldn't know it, but Higgins didn't consider six biscuits to be a full break-fast, not even when he had spread a fair bit of jam on each one of those biscuits and eaten some of the sour cabbage besides.

The problem, Jake realized, was that his friends knew his marriage to Elizabeth was a sham. They'd seen that he wasn't bedding down with her and they had sense enough to figure that, come spring, Elizabeth would be looking for a new husband.

A woman who could cook as fine as Elizabeth wouldn't need to look farther than this table for a husband to replace him.

It was all Jake could do to sit and act as if nothing was wrong.

And Elizabeth wasn't helping any. She kept bringing this to the table and that to the table. She should be sitting down beside him and showing the world that they were bound in holy wedlock. He had left the chair to his right free for her and he'd had to pull up a stump for himself to do so.

Obviously, his bride wasn't one to settle in quickly, though.

"Have a seat before the biscuits get cold," Jake finally said. If Elizabeth was going to marry a trapper come spring, it would be him. He might be willing to let her go to a rich man in some city who could give her all the comforts she deserved, but he wasn't willing to let her go to someone like him unless it *was* him.

"But—" Elizabeth started to protest.

"If there's anything else that needs to be brought to the table, you can tell me where it is and I'll get it," Jake said as he stood up. He thought he heard his new wife gasp in amazement, but he wasn't sure. He was too busy pulling the chair out for her so he could show Higgins how a real gentleman acted.

Elizabeth sat down. She wasn't used to sitting down with company. When she'd cooked for Matthew, they had sat together. But for years, she'd been working in the kitchen, or serving at the table, until the family meal was over and then she'd just eaten a few leftovers as she heated water to wash the dishes. She looked at the two men who still sat at the table and then at Spotted Fawn over by the fireplace. Elizabeth wasn't sure she knew what to say to any of them.

"Do you think I could learn?" Higgins asked.

It took a second for Elizabeth to realize what the man was talking about. "To be a gentleman? Of course."

"Teach me." Higgins asked and then seemed to reconsider. "I mean, I'd appreciate it mightily if you would be so kind." He stopped and then added, "Ma'am."

Higgins looked at her triumphantly.

"Well, I—"

"What kind of nonsense is this?" Wells demanded. He looked bewildered. "You planning to take up banking or something?"

"Women appreciate gentlemen," Higgins stated calmly.

Wells just looked at his friend. "What women?"

"Women. That's all. Just women."

"Women appreciate the kind of money we're making, that's what women appreciate."

"Not all women," Higgins said.

Elizabeth finally understood. "I'd be happy to give you some pointers." Somehow that didn't seem to be enough. "And I must say I think your efforts will pay off."

"You do?" Higgins looked over at her with the most hopeful look on his face.

Elizabeth nodded. "I most assuredly do."

The room was very silent. Elizabeth realized that not everyone knew about Annabelle Bliss or, if they did, they hadn't made the connections. She didn't want to give away any secrets. "Any woman would be pleased."

By now, Higgins was beaming.

Jake dropped a plate. Fortunately, it wasn't anything but a tin plate. He couldn't believe his ears. He'd taken

Elizabeth for a quiet, serious-minded woman. She hadn't seemed to want to take a second husband when she'd taken him. And here she was lining up another one—Higgins.

"We have a busy day ahead," Jake finally said. He didn't want to suggest Higgins and Wells leave, but he didn't want them to stay right now, either.

All pairs of eyes turned toward him. He'd just put a bit more wood in the stove.

"We have to unload the wagon," he explained.

"Oh, we could help with that," Higgins offered. "Sort of a thank-you. Nothing to it."

Jake clenched his jaw. "I can unload the wagon myself."

"When we get it unloaded, I thought maybe we should go back into town to the mercantile," Elizabeth said. "We'll need some things for Spotted Fawn before she goes to school."

Jake noticed his niece flinch at that news. She looked at him pleadingly.

Suddenly, it didn't seem so important whether or not he could show Higgins who was the better gentleman. Elizabeth wouldn't be settling down with either one of them anyway. If she had any sense, she'd be looking for some refined man from town by the time spring came.

The new Miles City banker, Harold Walls, was a widower and likely open to the prospect of marrying again. Or the man who had come here to open the hotel. What was his name? Well, it didn't matter. Both men were rich and traveled back East whenever the fancy took them. Jake couldn't compete financially with either one of them.

Then he looked at his niece. He had other things to worry about anyway. "Maybe we could get some lemon drops, too. I've heard the children in school all like lemon drops. They probably wouldn't say no if someone were to offer them one."

"I don't need to go to school," Spotted Fawn said. "I can talk English."

"You'll want to learn how to read," Jake said softly. "I know you have your father's Bible."

His niece didn't answer.

"I wish I knew how to read," Higgins finally said. "You don't want to pass up a chance to learn something like that."

"It won't be so bad," Elizabeth said. "You'll get used to it."

Spotted Fawn nodded slowly. "I'll try."

"Maybe we all should go into town," Elizabeth said brightly. "I didn't ask the reverend what you'll need for your first day in school. I'm sure they'll know at the mercantile, though."

"Well, let's get the wagon unloaded then," Higgins said.

Jake didn't refuse the offer this time. If Higgins was determined to help, he would let him. At least, he'd be able to watch the man if they were unloading the wagon together.

Elizabeth was worried. Jake said there was room in the lean-to for most of the goods in her wagon. But, as she recalled what she had there, she tried to remember where she had packed her sewing needles. It would take her at least a day to make Spotted Fawn ready for school. The girl would need to wear pantalettes instead of those pelts she had wrapped around her legs. The mercantile might have some ready-made ones that weren't too dear. And she'd also need shoes and stockings. Hopefully, they would have some that fit.

But a new dress for the girl would require some sewing. Even if Elizabeth only put tucks in one of her dresses for the girl to wear, it would take time. She might think of a dye to freshen up the one dress the girl did have, too.

It wasn't until everyone was ready to leave for Miles City, that Elizabeth remembered Annabelle, and Higgins's plans to be a gentleman.

"Maybe you should stop by the barbershop first," Elizabeth said to Higgins as Jake was helping her into the wagon.

The man was on his horse, preparing to ride along with them. "Why?"

"Women like a man with tidy hair," she said.

"I've never been to a barbershop," Wells offered with a frown. "Your hair just grows back if you get it cut, anyway."

"Yes, but it grows back more neatly. If you can't find a barber in Miles City, I'll cut your hair for you."

Elizabeth had cut Matthew's hair for him. She wasn't as good as a barber, but she'd managed.

"Maybe some other day," Wells said hesitantly. "Higgins is the one who wants to get all fancy. Me, I'm heading back home."

* * *

Jake wondered how he could have been so blind. It only took one look at Elizabeth bending her head toward Annabelle in the mercantile to know that something was up. Another look at Higgins's intensely still face as he watched them through the window told Jake all he needed to know. Higgins wasn't aiming for Elizabeth; he had his heart set on the woman behind the counter inside.

Jake felt relieved for himself, but more than anxious for his friend. He remembered when the three of them— Higgins, Wells and him—had fought off some hostile Blackfeet. They'd been holed up in the Paha Sapa, what some called the Black Hills, for several days and they were running out of ammunition and water. But, even facing death as they were, Higgins hadn't looked as miserable as he did now as the two of them stood on the porch outside the mercantile and tried not to look in through the window.

That, Jake told himself, was what a woman could do to a brave man.

He took another look at the inside of the store to be sure Spotted Fawn looked comfortable where she sat in the corner with the baby. Elizabeth had already told him she'd need a good hour to finish her business. Then he turned to Higgins.

"Come on, let's go find out if there's a barber in this town." Jake put his arm around his friend's shoulders. "How bad can it be to get a haircut anyway?"

A half hour later, Jake and Higgins walked back out on the street. The morning was almost over and there were people stepping every which way, going into one shop or another.

"I've been scalped," Higgins protested as he reached up to touch what little hair he had left. They still stood under the overhang that covered the walkway in front of the barber's shop.

Jake had to admit Higgins looked awfully pink all of a sudden. The man hadn't done more than trim his beard in the years Jake had known him. Now he was fresh-shaven and short-haired. Why, the man's forehead was pure white because it hadn't seen the sun in decades.

"You look younger," Jake offered by way of consolation. He decided not to mention the fact that the man's nose was a lot darker now than the rest of his face.

"Who wants to look younger?" Higgins bellowed. "Women are supposed to like a man who's been around awhile."

That stopped half of the people walking down the street. At least five women turned around and looked at Higgins. The man turned beet-red, which apparently didn't make him any more appealing to the women since they all turned back around and continued on their way a little faster than before.

"Neatness. That's what women like," Jake said as he rubbed his own neck. He was used to his hair being back there and now there was only air. His hair was cut short enough to compete with that new banker. Of course, Jake's neck was cold and probably white, too.

Higgins grunted. "I suppose I'll need to get new boots."

Jake nodded. "And a new hat."

Rightfully speaking, Higgins didn't have a hat now. It was little more than a buckskin bandana he'd used to tie his hair back. It had looked fine when the man had long hair, but it did look odd now.

"It's an expensive business—" Higgins frowned "—being a gentleman."

"I can't argue with that."

Somehow, though, Jake thought the other man didn't really mind.

Elizabeth had to look twice before she recognized Higgins when he stepped into the mercantile. If it weren't for the size of him, she might have needed to look a few more times. No one else was as massive and his height gave him away when his face didn't.

"Clarence?" Annabelle whispered from where she stood behind her counter.

Higgins's face went so pale even his nose was white. "I told you I don't use that name anymore."

Then Jake stepped into the mercantile, too. He chuckled. "I always wondered what the *C* stood for. I didn't think it was for Captain."

"It could have been," Higgins protested. "I helped the army out some."

"Oh." Elizabeth stared at Jake. It had taken her a minute to find her voice. "You cut your hair, too."

Jake's hair was still shining black, but now it had a few waves in it and it framed his face. Someone needed to smooth the strands into place, Elizabeth thought, but it wouldn't be her. She held her hands firmly at her sides.

Jake looked at her and smiled. "I figured I couldn't let Higgins make a fool of himself all alone."

"It's not foolish," Annabelle protested hotly from where she stood. "Good grooming is the mark of a gentleman."

Elizabeth took her eyes off Jake long enough to see Higgins swell up like a peacock. She'd noticed Annabelle had added a pretty brooch to her dress today, too. And set the bun on the back of her head a little higher so she'd look a little younger. The other woman had also greeted Elizabeth as if she knew she would be here today so she may have been hoping to see Higgins, as well.

"Thank you for noticing," Higgins finally said to Annabelle.

Jake gave a soft snort, not loud enough for Annabelle to hear, but he'd walked close enough to Elizabeth so she heard it.

"Do you need more time?" Jake asked as he stepped closer yet.

"No, but thank you for being gentleman enough to ask," she replied softly with a grin and watched Jake's eyes light up with laughter.

Annabelle and Higgins were having a moment of their own.

"You're just afraid of what Higgins and I would do if we had more time in town."

Elizabeth laughed. "Even so, I've finished with my shopping."

"You got the lemon drops?"

She nodded. "And a paper tablet with some lead pencils."

Elizabeth didn't mention that Annabelle had whispered to her that Mrs. Barker had been in with a petition, trying to get as many parents to sign it as she could. She wanted to prevent Spotted Fawn from going to school with the other children. Fortunately, she hadn't had many signatures when Annabelle saw it. Maybe the other adults in Miles City would decide it was only fair that Jake's niece have a chance to have the same kind of schooling that their children had.

The parents would think that, too, if they could have seen the girl earlier as she sat in the mercantile waiting patiently for Elizabeth to finish talking with Annabelle. It wasn't until they were almost done that Elizabeth noticed the girl had been holding open a small Bible. She clearly couldn't read, but she seemed to be trying.

Elizabeth wondered how many of the white children in Miles City had that much of a longing to read God's Word. She was glad Annabelle had seen the girl, too. Maybe that information could circulate around the town along with the petition.

Chapter Seven

Jake was happy as he sat near the fireplace and whittled. He couldn't help but notice that his wife looked happy, too. Elizabeth never referred to herself as his wife, but he found he liked calling her that, even if it was only in his mind. He had begun praying that Elizabeth would grow content with her life here.

He was watching her now as she stood in the light of the coal oil lamp and twisted pieces of old rags into Spotted Fawn's long black hair. The baby was already in her crib sleeping. Maybe it was all of the effort Elizabeth was putting into getting the baby fed and Spotted Fawn ready for school that was causing the good feelings he was having.

Marrying Elizabeth O'Brian was the best thing he'd ever done, Jake told himself as he paused in his movements. Four different hair ribbons were spread out on the table. The final decision had not yet been made on which one they would use. He doubted Spotted Fawn had ever worn a ribbon before and he knew he wouldn't have thought to get her ribbons if it wasn't for Elizabeth guiding them.

It didn't matter if this woman had come from the East or the West, whether she was used to a soft life or a hard life. She was the woman his family needed; she belonged with them.

Even his niece seemed to know it.

"You'll be the prettiest girl in school tomorrow," Jake said as he smiled over at Spotted Fawn, who was sitting in a chair pulled up to the table. She had an old apron tied around her shoulders. She was the only one in the room who didn't look happy.

"She's better off not being the prettiest," Elizabeth said mildly as she wrapped another strand of hair. "She doesn't need to call any attention to herself. We've already talked about it and, the first day, she's just going to smile a lot."

Spotted Fawn looked up at him and gave him a smile that was almost a grimace.

"She should just be herself," Jake said. "The other kids will like her when they get a chance to know her."

"I'm sure they will."

Elizabeth didn't look at him when she said that and Jake had a sinking feeling that his wife didn't think Spotted Fawn would have an easy time of it in school. Elizabeth had told him about the petition Mrs. Barker had been passing around, but he assumed the woman hadn't gotten many signatures or someone would have been out to his place to tell him about it by now.

"We'll take you to school and see that everything's okay," Jake said.

Elizabeth looked over at him.

"We'll stop by after Spotted Fawn has settled in a bit," Elizabeth corrected him as she made one last knot in a rag and patted the girl on the shoulder. "There, you're all ready for bed now. Have sweet dreams and don't worry about anything."

Spotted Fawn looked over at Jake with a question in her eyes.

He nodded. "I'll be up in a minute to say your prayers with you."

Red Tail had always said evening prayers with Spotted Fawn and Jake knew that was the time when his niece missed her parents the most.

Spotted Fawn stood up and Elizabeth took the apron off of the girl's shoulders. For a second, Jake had thought Elizabeth was going to bend down and kiss the top of his niece's head. But she didn't.

Spotted Fawn was waiting for something, though.

Elizabeth looked down at the girl. With her hair in rags and the worried expression on her face, Spotted Fawn looked a lot like Elizabeth had felt at her age when she needed to walk to a new household to see if she could work there for a while. Everything always depended on the kindness of the women in the new place. She supposed it would be the same for Spotted Fawn.

"The day will go fast," Elizabeth said softly as she reached over to smooth down a stray piece of the girl's hair that had escaped a knotted rag. "And I'm going to bake some molasses cookies to put in your lunch pail."

In the two days that she and Spotted Fawn had been getting ready for school, Elizabeth had discovered that the girl liked cookies. Elizabeth planned to bake some before the stove cooled off tonight.

Spotted Fawn nodded to Elizabeth before turning to the ladder that led up to the loft.

Elizabeth watched as the girl climbed the ladder.

"Here." Jake walked over and pulled out a chair for Elizabeth. "Rest a bit before you worry about those cookies."

Elizabeth nodded as she eased herself into the chair. It had been a long day. "I hope—" She looked at the loft above. Spotted Fawn was already up there.

Jake nodded. "Me, too."

Elizabeth could hear Spotted Fawn moving around in the loft.

"We can't go with her to school, though," Elizabeth murmured quietly so they wouldn't be overheard. "The other kids will tease her if we do."

"Well, what do other parents do?"

Jake looked so bewildered, Elizabeth started to giggle. "I'm sure I don't know."

Elizabeth couldn't get her breath. She knew it was half from exhaustion, but the more she giggled the more Jake's eyes danced along with her. She liked watching the lamplight flicker on his face. He was standing beside her chair, looking down at her, and then—

Oh, my, Jake had bent down and was kissing her. She

should pull away and say something, but she couldn't think of anything coherent to say. This kiss was—no, she was. Everything stopped. Yes, she was a bad woman.

"You're not supposed to do that," Elizabeth finally whispered as she managed to pull away slightly.

She remembered, of course, that he had kissed her when the minister pronounced them married, but that had been a kiss with a purpose. A wedding kiss had a certain dignity to it. But this—this kiss was something a grieving widow should never be part of.

Matthew and her baby had only been dead for fifteen days. What was wrong with her? They were cold in the ground and she was—she'd never felt this way before.

Elizabeth couldn't look at Jake, but she saw him stand up anyway.

"Don't worry," he said. "I'll leave—I—"

"You can't leave. You have to pray with Spotted Fawn."

Elizabeth kept her gaze on the table, but she eventually saw Jake start walking toward the ladder that went up to the loft.

Elizabeth was glad when he'd climbed to the top.

She wanted some peace while she contemplated what was wrong with her. Maybe all the time that Matthew had been grumbling because she wasn't enough of a lady to suit him, he wasn't talking about her hair or her clothes. Maybe he had been able to see inside of her and he realized she was a wanton. A loose woman.

She had never suspected. She had known she had to be very careful in the households where she worked. People all too often assumed servant girls had no morals. But she had always thought the problem was with other people. She had never expected to feel this heat rising up within herself.

Elizabeth listened to the sounds of Jake and Spotted Fawn praying together. How could he talk to God after this? He had promised to respect her grief. She had been Matthew's wife and she'd been on the verge of betraying his memory. The worst of it was that she had never been stirred like this with Matthew.

It wasn't until she heard the voices upstairs fade away that she stood up. She had cookies to bake before she went to bed. It was her gift to Spotted Fawn—something to give the girl comfort in the middle of the day tomorrow. It would remind her that people were at home thinking of her.

Jake sat up in the loft until Spotted Fawn closed her eyes. He could hear Elizabeth moving around downstairs and he thought he should give her some peace. He had blundered badly. He had seen the shocked distress on her face.

The problem was he'd neglected to court his wife. He was feeling married to her, even if he had no right to it. But he should have remembered she didn't feel the same about him.

He had noticed earlier in the afternoon that she was marking the days beside her bed as she had done beside her tent. He'd even counted the days she had there, but he had not realized what all of those lines in the dirt meant. Elizabeth still marked her life by the death of her husband. God might not be sending her the fever, but she considered herself tied to that family she'd buried in a way that left no room for him and his nieces.

He slowly climbed down the rope ladder. Elizabeth stood by the stove. The room smelled of ginger and molasses.

"Thank you for all you did today," Jake said quietly. Even if she didn't have room in her heart for him and his nieces, she was doing her duty by them. That was more than a lot of women would do. Come spring, he'd have to find a way to let her go if that's what she wanted.

Elizabeth didn't turn around as Jake walked out of the cabin. She was ashamed to face herself; she certainly didn't want her emotions to be seen by anyone else.

She finished baking the cookies. Then the baby woke up, hungry to be fed.

Elizabeth held the baby as it nursed. Everything always seemed better when she had the baby in her arms. The little one was gaining weight and making happy gurgling sounds that made Elizabeth smile.

The baby fell back asleep before Elizabeth returned her to the crib.

The house was warm and quiet again before Elizabeth went to bed. She didn't sleep well, but she hadn't expected to. Finally, she got up early. She wanted to make certain that the cabin was warm for Spotted Fawn when she dressed. Elizabeth had already decided that she would react to Jake as though nothing had happened last night. She didn't want Spotted Fawn to be any more worried than she already was.

Besides, the problem didn't lie within Jake; it lay within her. She was the one who had forgotten her husband.

When Spotted Fawn came down the ladder, Elizabeth put all worries out of her mind. Yesterday, she'd helped Spotted Fawn try on each new piece of clothing. Now, of course, the girl didn't like anything she was supposed to wear.

"I'll be cold," Spotted Fawn complained as she stood by the bed. Elizabeth was holding out the white linen pantalettes. Fortunately, the mercantile had some that were only a little large on the girl.

"You'll have an extra petticoat."

Black lace-up boots were sitting on one of the table chairs and the blue calico dress that Elizabeth had cut down from one of hers was hanging on the back of the rocking chair.

"I'm sorry, but you can't wear your leggings," Elizabeth said when Spotted Fawn kept frowning at the pantalettes.

Leggings wasn't the right term, but Elizabeth refused to call them animal pelts although that was what they really were. They had been Elizabeth's biggest challenge. She knew Spotted Fawn didn't stand a chance of being accepted by the other children unless she dressed like them and the leggings were the most obvious difference in her usual clothes. To make matters worse, the pelts had been rubbed with bear grease, probably to keep out the dampness, and had a strong animal smell.

When they'd gone to the mercantile earlier, Elizabeth

had picked out a length of yellow calico to make another dress for Spotted Fawn. She'd start sewing on that this afternoon. And she'd see about dyeing the girl's old dress. Elizabeth had enough dried leaves and things to work with until she could grow the plants she usually used for her dyeing.

"Why don't you pick out your ribbon while I get the biscuits out of the oven?" Elizabeth suggested. The ribbons were the one thing that Spotted Fawn had liked about her new wardrobe.

Elizabeth wasn't surprised when Spotted Fawn picked the red one. The girl loved that color. After Jake came inside and they ate breakfast, Elizabeth tied the ribbon around Spotted Fawn's hair.

They had agreed they would all ride into Miles City in the wagon early enough to get Spotted Fawn to school on time. But Jake and Elizabeth would wait a couple of hours before stopping by the schoolhouse to see how things were going for the girl.

It was almost two hours after the school bell had initially rung that Jake looked up from the newspaper he was reading. He was sitting on a chair in a corner of the mercantile while Elizabeth stood over by the counter, looking at some dress patterns and chatting quietly with Annabelle. Fortunately, someone must have explained to Annabelle that Jake wasn't a wolfer because she had been cordial to him this morning.

"Do they ring the bell again for recess?" Jake asked as he stood up.

"Sometimes," Annabelle said. "I think it's up to the reverend."

"Is it time for us to go over?" Elizabeth looked up at him.

"I'd guess they are out to recess about now so it'd be as good a time as any to say hello to her."

Elizabeth nodded and put the pattern she was looking at back in the box on the counter. They both said goodbye to Annabelle and then they walked out of the store.

Jake heard the sound of children laughing as they walked down the street toward the schoolhouse so he figured he'd timed it about right for recess. Maybe if all of the kids were outside, he'd be able to ask the reverend how Spotted Fawn had done this morning. She knew how to speak English, but she'd be at the beginning of the McGuffey Reader they used in the school. He wondered if he shouldn't have tried to teach Spotted Fawn how to read a little bit before she went to school.

Jake heard a girl's scream and then a yell— *"Ho'ka hey."*

"What was *that?*" Elizabeth asked as she looked around.

Jake started to run. "The Lakota battle cry."

He heard Elizabeth's footsteps following him.

The reverend was coming out of the schoolhouse as Jake reached the steps.

"Where's Spotted Fawn?" he asked the other man.

"Behind the school with the other children. It's recess."

"Not any longer," Jake said as he started to run around the school.

Jake came to a stop when he reached the area behind the school. There were a few scrub trees close by, but the children were all standing still as though they were afraid to move. In the middle of them all, Spotted Fawn was crouched down with a wild look in her eyes and a small branch in her outstretched hand.

"What happened here?" Jake asked as he slowly walked toward Spotted Fawn. He knew she had times when she remembered her village being burned by some soldiers, but he hadn't expected this.

"My ma says we don't need to go to school with no Injuns," one of the taller boys said. He had flaming red hair which could only mean one thing: he was a Barker.

Jake didn't pay him any attention. He squatted down to be level with his niece. "Spotted Fawn?"

His niece looked up at him and, as she moved her arms, he saw the egg that had been thrown at the front of her new dress. Her face was dirty and she had a bruise on her cheek. Her red ribbon was missing and her hair swung around in disarray, the curls all gone.

"Elias Barker, you go inside this minute," the Reverend Olson's voice thundered behind Jake. "Mary, you go get Mrs. Barker for me. We're going to get this settled right now. I won't have my students caught up in a brawl."

"Well, it was her fault," Elias said.

"I doubt that very much," the reverend said as he pointed to the schoolhouse. "And if I find out that you're the one that started this, you're going to be cleaning blackboards for the rest of your natural life."

Jake saw Elias walk back to the schoolhouse at the same time as Elizabeth bent down beside him. She'd found the red ribbon somewhere.

"Here, let's get you cleaned up," Elizabeth said as she offered a hand to Spotted Fawn. "I'm sure Annabelle will let us use her room so you can get rid of this dirt."

Jake had thought Elizabeth had taken care of his nieces earlier. But it was nothing compared to what she was doing now. She helped Spotted Fawn get up and put her arm around the girl's shoulder as if they were going for a stroll somewhere. She made everything look so dignified.

Elizabeth turned to look at the reverend. "We'll be back as soon as we can."

The reverend nodded. "Rest assured, I'll have the class ready to apologize by the time you do."

Elizabeth nodded as she walked away with Spotted Fawn.

Jake still felt like pounding something. He settled for glaring at the two older boys who stood there smirking.

"What was that?" a nearby girl asked Jake and he wondered what she meant.

"That thing Spotted Fawn said," the girl persisted. "What does it mean?"

"That it's a good day to die. The Lakota Sioux say that when they ride into battle." Jake looked over and noticed the boys weren't smirking any longer.

"That doesn't make them come here, does it?" one of the boys asked. "The Indians, I mean. It's not like *calling* them here, is it?"

Jake hid a grin as he shrugged. "You'll have to ask Spotted Fawn."

Jake wished adults could be told to stay after school the way their children could. Mrs. Barker wasn't doing anything to encourage peace in the classroom. Fortunately, the Reverend Olson had asked the rest of the children, even Elias, to stay outside while the adults had their meeting.

"I told you there would be trouble," Mrs. Barker said the minute the three adults were inside and the door was closed. "That girl doesn't belong here."

"Your son started the trouble."

"Indians have no place in the Miles City School."

"You don't own the school," Jake said.

"Neither do you."

Mrs. Barker stood in the school aisle with her hands on her hips and Jake felt his temper rising.

"Now, now," the reverend said as he came back from closing the door. "We need to talk about this rationally."

"I am being perfectly rational," Mrs. Barker said as she pointed at Jake. "He's the one who isn't moving ahead with the times. This isn't Indian country any longer. Those savages have no place here."

"My niece is going to this school and if you try to stop it I'll call in my loan on the lumber."

Mrs. Barker turned to the reverend. "Can he do that?"

Reverend Olson nodded. "It's his right. Half of the lumber in the school is his."

The woman turned around to face Jake. "The school can't afford that."

"I know."

"Well, your niece can sit on *your* side of the school then, but my son will sit on the town's side."

With that the woman turned and walked out of the school.

"Well, I guess that is a compromise," the reverend said hesitantly. "Or at least moving in that direction. She said Spotted Fawn can be here."

Jake grunted. He wasn't sure what was going on in Mrs. Barker's head, but he didn't think it was compromise.

Chapter Eight

Elizabeth used her fork to pick up a piece of cooked carrot. Jake had invited her to have a roast beef dinner with him in the hotel. Of course, she knew the invitation was just an excuse for them to linger in town until it was time for school to be dismissed. Neither one of them had wanted to return Spotted Fawn to school unless they were close enough to help if there were problems later.

"We should have pie, too," Jake suggested. His new hat sat on the chair next to him and Elizabeth sat across the table from him. He didn't even seem to notice that the waitress had stopped to ask several times if he'd like her to put his wonderful new hat on the rack by the door. *Wonderful*, Elizabeth thought sourly. That was the waitress's exact word. A hat wasn't wonderful.

"Pie would be nice," Elizabeth said. She needed to forget about Jake's hat and enjoy herself.

The hotel had maroon rugs spread along its floors

and white linen napkins on the tables. The silver was heavy and well-polished. Elizabeth had never been in such a fine place to eat. Then the waitress came back. It seemed she was not only worried about Jake's hat; she also seemed to be offering him more coffee than the other diners.

Not that Elizabeth was jealous, she assured herself. She just didn't want the young woman to exert herself for nothing. Elizabeth put her hand on top of the table and turned the ring on her finger slightly so it would catch more of the light shining in the window.

There—by the look on the woman's face, the waitress had finally noticed.

Elizabeth put her hand back on her lap. She liked the feel of the wedding band on her finger, although she was no longer sure if the ring reminded her of Matthew or of Jake. Not that it mattered. She planned to give Matthew the widow's respect that he was due. Not that she wanted women flirting with her other husband, either.

Oh, dear. She winced as she heard herself thinking. Was she that confused?

"I suppose you'd like to read some this winter," Jake said.

"What?" Elizabeth looked up from her plate. Why would he ask that? "I've always worked hard. Summer or winter."

She couldn't blame the waitress for noticing that Jake was the most handsome man in the room. He'd shaved again this morning and his short hair was falling into place nicely. The waitress was probably not the only woman here who had wondered about him.

Right now, he was leaning toward her, though. "I'm just saying that we could buy a book or two at the mercantile. This might be a good time to see what they have in stock. A home should have a few books for reading."

"Oh." Elizabeth guessed that made sense. She'd never had any leisure for reading anything but the Bible. "Maybe there'd be a book we could read with Spotted Fawn."

"And poetry. We could get some poetry, too—that is, if you'd like it. I know women like their words."

"Yes, yes, of course." Elizabeth tried not to let her dismay show. She had learned how to read here and there in her life, but she'd never sat down with a book of poetry. She wasn't even sure she could read all those fancy words if she saw them. "If that's what you'd like."

"I…" Jake opened his mouth and then closed it again.

Elizabeth thought he looked frustrated. "I suppose you're worried about…things."

"What things?"

"Well, I imagine me and the girls are keeping you from your work."

"It's winter. I don't prospect in the winter. I think the Black Hills are pretty well played out anyway."

"Well, that's too bad." Elizabeth reached for the water glass at the top of her plate. "I guess."

Just then the waitress came to ask if they'd like some apple pie. At least this time she offered both of them cream on their pie.

They ate for a few minutes in silence.

Jake lingered over his dessert. He was trying to think of ways to court Elizabeth and he wasn't being too successful. He tried to remember if there had been any romantic gestures between his parents. He knew his father had gone to great trouble to bring a few of his mother's possessions out West with them. It was her rocking chair that Jake had in his cabin now. His mother had been very grateful to his father for keeping the chair with them. And his father had sent back East once for some lilac perfume that had delighted his mother. She said a lady needed her perfume. Even if his mother returned to her unhappiness, those presents brightened her life for a time.

Maybe that's something he could do. "Is rose your favorite scent, too?"

Elizabeth looked up from her plate. She'd just taken the last bite of her pie.

"I mean, I know you're partial to the flower," Jake continued. "I was just wondering about the smell of them. Like in perfume."

"Rose water is lovely," Elizabeth said hesitantly.

Jake nodded. "We'll get some of that, too, then."

Elizabeth looked puzzled now. "You mean for Spotted Fawn? I'm not sure girls would wear rose water. Especially not to school. Mostly they just wash up good."

"No, I mean for you."

"Me? But I—I—"

Jake could tell he'd gone about this wrong. "You smell wonderful all by yourself. I just thought you'd like a present."

Now Elizabeth was looking at him suspiciously. "You already got me a present. The teapot."

"Well, but Christmas is coming up. The teapot is your wedding present. It can't be your Christmas present, too."

"Oh, I forgot. Yes, Christmas. It must almost be December."

All of Elizabeth's reserve melted away and she beamed at him with pure delight on her face.

"It's December third." He wondered what she'd be like on Christmas Day if the mere thought of the holiday brought out such sparkle to her eyes.

"Well, some rose water would be very nice then," she agreed. "I'll need to get you a present, too. And the girls, of course."

Jake nodded. He wished someone had told him how hard this courting business would be. He suddenly had a lot of sympathy with his father as he tried to please his wife. He wondered if he should warn Higgins.

Just then the man himself appeared.

"Annabelle told me where to find the two of you," the man said as he drew up a chair and sat down at the table with them. "She also told me what those kids did. Those boys should be turned over someone's knee. And I wouldn't mind doing the turning."

"Reverend Olson will handle it," Jake said.

Higgins snorted. "The Reverend doesn't stand a chance with boys like that. I know, I used to be one of them. They'll convince him to forgive them and then they'll be at it again."

Jake didn't answer. He wasn't sure if the reverend would be able to persuade the boys to behave or not. The reverend was a peacemaker and sometimes that didn't work so well with bullies.

"At least Annabelle asked her boy, Thomas, to look out for Spotted Fawn," Higgins said. "He told her what had happened when he came home for lunch."

"Thomas isn't big enough to face those boys," Elizabeth said. "He's only ten. Some of those older boys are thirteen or fourteen."

Jake stood up. "Then maybe we should go see for ourselves."

The schoolhouse door was closed when Jake, Elizabeth, and Higgins walked down the street toward it. It was midafternoon and the sky was gray. The streets of Miles City were quiet. There weren't even any riders coming into town.

"We'll just peek in the window," Elizabeth said. None of them had gone up the steps yet. "I don't want the children to tease Spotted Fawn."

"Sounds to me like those boys already did that." Higgins grumbled.

"But no one has teased her about her parents yet," Elizabeth said. "And I don't want them to tease her about me."

Jake turned in astonishment and pushed his hat up so he could see his wife more clearly. She shouldn't be worried about people thinking badly of her because of him and the children. "How in the world could they tease her about *you?*"

Elizabeth raised her chin just a little. "The children

might know I'm the woman who was supposed to die of the fever. And, I was camped out in that tent by the fort. Who knows what people are saying about me? They probably think I'm crazy. And no girl that age wants anyone to think she can't make a move without her parents watching her. "

Jake jammed his hat back down on his head. Now, if that didn't beat all. "Well, I'm going to be watching no matter what she wants."

"Of course," Elizabeth said as she stepped up on the porch and slid closer to the window. "I never said we shouldn't watch over her. We just need to do it so no one notices. You know, tactfully."

"I can be tactful," Jake growled as he followed her up the steps.

Higgins snorted.

Elizabeth was the first one to peek in the window of the schoolhouse. Jake and Higgins stood to the side of her.

"Oh," she breathed softly when she got a clear view.

Elizabeth's heart sank. Spotted Fawn and Thomas were sitting all alone on one side of the classroom. The other children were all pushed together on the benches on the other side. The Reverend Olson was not looking happy, but he was pointing to something on the map.

Elizabeth stepped away from the window.

Jake didn't even ask what she'd seen. He just took a look himself. His face was grim when he stepped back to where Elizabeth was standing.

"It'll get better," Elizabeth whispered hopefully.

"It will after I go in there and talk some sense to those kids."

"That might make it worse. It's Friday today. By Monday the children will probably have forgotten all about this. But if we stir it up even more, it'll take longer to fix it."

"I suppose you're right," Jake said softly as he rubbed a hand over his head.

Neither one of them had noticed that Higgins had stepped away until they heard him knocking on the school door.

"What's he doing?" Jake turned to whisper.

Elizabeth could only shake her head. Whatever it was, they were too late to stop it.

"Hello, everyone," Higgins said as he opened the door to the schoolhouse. Elizabeth and Jake could hear him clearly as he walked into the room. "I'm here to sign up. I figure it's time I learned to read."

Elizabeth and Jake were silent for a moment.

"Well, at least he's not her parent," Jake finally said.

"And she'll be safe," Elizabeth added.

They just looked at each other for a moment before they turned and walked back to the mercantile.

They didn't talk much as they rode back home in the wagon. Then Jake went to check the animals and Elizabeth brought out the yellow calico she was going to use in Spotted Fawn's new dress. If she worked on it this evening and all of Saturday, she should have the dress ready for the girl to wear Sunday morning.

Elizabeth picked the sharpest one of her needles and

set it beside the fabric. Then she bowed her head. She hadn't been praying much lately. But she felt helpless in light of what she'd seen today. *Dear Father,* she prayed. *Help me to know what to do. Help me know what to say to Spotted Fawn. Don't let the bullies win.*

Elizabeth knew that the heartache she felt over Spotted Fawn was an echo of the things she had suffered in her own life as a child. The Bible said that God took care of the orphans, but she wasn't so sure. If He really cared so much, there wouldn't be any orphans to begin with. Or widows, either. Or mothers who lost their babies.

Her anger at God felt like ashes in her mouth. How could she be angry and need Him so much at the same time? She shook her head. She had no answers.

Spotted Fawn looked tired when she came home from school. Higgins walked her to the door and Elizabeth thanked him.

"My pleasure, ma'am," he said as he tipped his hat to her.

"How was the rest of the day at school?" Elizabeth asked Spotted Fawn after Higgins left.

The girl didn't say anything.

"Well, it'll be better on Monday," Elizabeth finally said. "Would you like some biscuits? We have some left from breakfast."

Spotted Fawn nodded as she sat down at the table. Elizabeth opened a jar of rhubarb jam and set it beside the girl with her biscuits. The girl made no move to eat, so Elizabeth sat down beside her.

Only then did Spotted Fawn pick up the biscuit.

Dinner was late because they were waiting for Jake. Elizabeth had fried some potatoes and salt pork.

"I want to go home," Spotted Fawn announced after they had all finished eating.

"But you are home," Jake protested.

"I want to be with my people."

"Oh, dear," Elizabeth said. She looked up and met Jake's gaze.

Jake cleared his throat softly. "I know it was hard for you today, but you can't go back to your people."

"The Crying One and I will go," the girl insisted. "I have my pony. My father taught me like the son he did not have."

"Well, you're certainly not just going off by yourself," Elizabeth said. That much she knew. "Who knows what kind of people you'd meet out there."

"I'd meet my people," Spotted Fawn said. "I'm not afraid."

"Your father knew you'd need to be brave to live in the white man's world," Jake said. "But he wanted you to live. Both you and your sister."

Spotted Fawn was silent.

"Please, give it another chance," Elizabeth said. "I know it's hard, but we'll think of a way."

Spotted Fawn nodded and left the table. She went to sit by where her sister was lying in the crib. The girl picked up the baby and hugged her before returning her to the crib.

"There's church on Sunday," Jake said as his niece walked toward her rope ladder. "Maybe by then people will have calmed down a bit. The kids will forget all about which side of the room they're sitting on."

Elizabeth nodded as she looked over at Jake. She wondered if he really believed that or if he was just saying it to give Spotted Fawn hope. Elizabeth knew how it felt to be unwelcome in a place. She had needed to work hard in some households to find any measure of acceptance. Of course, she had always softened people's hearts first with the food she cooked. People always seemed friendlier if they were biting into a biscuit or a fried apple doughnut.

Jake had been in the lean-to repairing his traps and, when he came next door, he smelled a mouthwatering aroma. There were jars on the table and the smell of cinnamon in the air. And something else.

"Doughnuts!" Jake couldn't believe it. Sometimes for breakfast, one of the restaurants in Miles City served doughnuts but they weren't anything like the perfectly round golden things that were sitting on several plates on the table. Spotted Fawn was standing beside the doughnuts, her dress covered by a large white apron that was too big for her. She had a cup of what looked like sugar in her hand and a streak of flour on her face.

She reached for a plate and held it out to him. Jake took one of the doughnuts and bit into it. He'd never tasted anything so good. There were pieces of apple in the dough. And the cinnamon and sugar that his niece was sprinkling on them gave each one an extra something. They were wonderful.

"We're making fried apple doughnuts," Spotted Fawn said proudly.

Elizabeth looked up from where she stood by the stove. "I thought we could take a big basket of them to church tomorrow to pass around. It might, you know, help people get along better."

Jake decided the doughnuts were not the sweetest thing in this room.

"I think that's a fine idea," he said, grinning.

Even Mrs. Barker wouldn't be able to make progress against a campaign like this. The adults in Miles City, most of them men, would rather eat a doughnut than sign a petition any day. And the children—Jake would bet even Elias might be willing to sit on the same side of the schoolroom with Spotted Fawn if he got to eat these doughnuts.

Chapter Nine

Jake reined in his team of horses, pulling the wagon off the street near the schoolhouse. When they had built the schoolhouse, they had placed it on the edge of Miles City so there would be room behind it for the children to play. It was Sunday morning and he, Elizabeth and the girls were preparing to go inside for the usual preaching service. It had snowed a little last night and the air was still moist, but he could already see smoke coming out of the chimney on the building's roof so it should be warm enough inside.

Someday, Miles City hoped to have its own church, but for now everyone sat on the benches the children used during the week for school. It was a little crowded and occasionally someone would get ink on their clothes, but no one seriously complained. It was better than meeting in a saloon as some of the churches in other small towns had to do.

Jake walked around the wagon and lifted his niece

to the ground before giving the baby to Spotted Fawn so he could help Elizabeth climb down.

"Wait," Elizabeth said after she shook out her skirts and took the baby back. "I want to be sure everyone is buttoned up and spotless."

Elizabeth gave Jake and his niece a final inspection that would have made the sergeants at the fort proud.

Jake had shaved earlier and he was wearing the blue shirt Elizabeth had washed and ironed for him. Spotted Fawn had a red ribbon neatly tied in her hair. The girl's new dress wasn't ready, but Jake thought the made-over calico looked respectable enough on her thin frame. And the bruise on her face barely showed now. She didn't have a coat, but Elizabeth had given her his best blanket to wrap around like a shawl.

In Jake's opinion his niece looked pretty good. She would look even better, of course, if she didn't have that haunted look in her eyes. Earlier, when they had sat around the table before eating breakfast, he'd prayed for all of them. He asked God to make the doughnuts a true peace offering to the children and parents in Miles City.

Jake said another quick prayer now. Spotted Fawn had seen too much violence in her young life. Any kind of anger made her withdraw; he prayed God would help her feel safe.

Right now, his niece was standing very still while Elizabeth did her inspection. It was clear Spotted Fawn wanted to please the woman who was helping them all.

Elizabeth brushed a speck of something off Spotted

Fawn's shoulder and then bent quickly to give the young girl a kiss on her forehead.

Spotted Fawn smiled slightly.

"We look fine," Elizabeth announced as she stood back up and gave a nod to Jake.

Jake couldn't agree more and he was only looking at one person. Elizabeth's gray dress made her eyes turn a deeper green and the resolve on her face moved his heart. He'd been wrong about her. She was nothing like his mother. She was already teaching Spotted Fawn some important lessons on how to face adversity. Elizabeth leaned into life, she didn't back away from it the way his mother had.

Jake took the baby so Elizabeth could carry the basket. He was proud of his family as they all walked up the steps of the schoolhouse. The sounds of voices reached them so he guessed a fair number of people were already gathering for the service. Normally, people kept their voices more subdued as they readied themselves for church, but it might be best if people were more relaxed today.

Even in the damp air, Jake could smell the doughnuts that Elizabeth was carrying in the basket. She had put a piece of red gingham on the bottom of the wicker basket and another one over the top. With her gray dress, it made everything look like a picnic.

When they reached the door, something about the voices inside the schoolhouse made Jake pause. The Reverend Olson had an early service for the soldiers at the fort so he wouldn't be here yet to do his civilian service. Generally, people did talk before he came, but these voices sounded sharper than usual. Instead of ushering Elizabeth in as he normally would, he stood in front of her as he opened the door.

"Whoa!" Jake recoiled as he saw what someone had done. The people inside were all standing around the edges of the room, looking uncomfortable and staring because, right there in the center of the schoolroom, from the front of the room to the back, someone had painted an ugly black stripe. The stripe divided the room in half. On one side, the painter had crudely lettered *Miles City.* And on the other, he or she had painted the words, *Dry Creek.*

Jake closed the door as quickly as he could and faced his family. "We're going home."

"What's wrong?" Elizabeth asked as she turned with him.

Jake shifted the baby he was holding so he could guide Spotted Fawn and Elizabeth with his other arm. "I'm taking all of you to the wagon. You can wait there while I talk to some people about something."

Elizabeth hesitated for a minute and then reached out her arms to take the baby from Jake. "We can manage. I'll take the girls and we'll wait for you there."

By now, Jake saw his friend Higgins riding into town at a slow gallop. Then he saw Wells, pounding hard behind him. They were clearly heading for the schoolhouse, even though they'd never shown any interest in going to any of the church services that had been held there in recent months.

Virginia and Annabelle were starting out into the street, but they held back to let Higgins and Wells pass.

"Go to Elizabeth," Jake called out to the women as he pointed to his wife.

Then he turned his attention to the men.

Higgins pulled his horse to a stop beside Jake. "You been inside?"

Jake nodded. "Enough to see what's been done. How did you know?"

"Annabelle sent Tommy out to tell us. He's putting his pony away now. We figured you might need some help."

Jake looked over at the wagon. He couldn't make out what any of the women were saying, but his heart sank when he saw the hand gestures Annabelle was making. She was clearly telling Elizabeth about the black dividing line. His earlier words about half of the school lumber being his must have prompted someone to do this. Even without the hand gestures, he would have known what was being said by how stiff Elizabeth's back became.

Higgins and Wells both climbed off their horses.

"Well," Higgins said as he rolled up the sleeves on his shirt. "Do we divide the room into three? I'll take the men on the right. Wells can take the middle. We'll show them what Dry Creek people are made of."

Jake shook his head. "It's a church. Besides, violence isn't the answer."

"Violence was sure the answer when it came to the classroom," Higgins protested. "I told Elias Barker that he'd be sorrier than a treed cat if he ever did anything to Spotted Fawn again. Then I gave him my grizzly growl. The boy turned white enough that I figure he got the message."

"He might have heard what you said, but it didn't change his mind so it didn't really solve anything," Jake said as he pointed to the wood-frame structure in front of them. "Just like all the talking I've been doing. And now we've got the line right across the room in there."

All of the men stood and looked at the building.

"Don't seem fair that we can't fight because it's a church," Wells finally said. "It's a schoolhouse most of the time."

"You shouldn't fight in a schoolhouse, either," Elizabeth said as she walked up behind them. "Besides, it's nothing to be afraid of. It's only a bit of paint."

Jake hadn't realized Elizabeth was there. He turned to look at her.

"Oh, I know its meanness and spite at the same time," Elizabeth added. Her jaw was set and her eyes blazed with determination. "But we can't just go home and let them win. What kind of a message does that send to the children of this town?"

Jake realized he hadn't been thinking about the other children. He just wanted to protect Spotted Fawn. Like it or not, though, those children would be his niece's classmates. And maybe her neighbors for the rest of her life. Letting someone get away with that black line was bad for the whole town.

"Hey, something sure smells good," Wells said.

Spotted Fawn had just walked up with the basket of

doughnuts. Annabelle and Virginia were walking beside the girl.

"It's our doughnuts," Spotted Fawn said. "Elizabeth says they're a peace offering."

Spotted Fawn looked up at him with a fragile hope in her eyes and Jake realized he needed to say something to encourage his niece. "If Elizabeth thinks they'll bring peace, we'll give it a try, won't we?"

Spotted Fawn gave a slight nod and then she looked over at Elizabeth.

If Jake hadn't seen it with his own eyes, he wouldn't have believed it. But he watched as Spotted Fawn squared her shoulders and then lifted her chin in the exact same way Elizabeth had done just seconds ago.

Jake might have a dozen enemies on the other side of that school door, but his heart was warm just the same. Maybe an Eastern lady had something to offer his nieces that he hadn't expected. He knew she had plenty to offer him.

This time, Jake opened the door so that he and Elizabeth could enter the schoolhouse together. Elizabeth carried the baby and Spotted Fawn, with her basket, followed close behind. By now, folks had sorted themselves out and were sitting on the Miles City side of the stripe. The benches were empty on the Dry Creek side.

Usually, people didn't even seat themselves this early. They stood and talked with each other until the reverend came. Jake would guess the good man wouldn't be here for another five minutes and maybe longer the way the roads were since the light snow that fell last night had already melted and turned the ground soft.

There were muddy footprints on the floor and the smell of wet wool in the air. Someone would have to scrub the floor before school tomorrow, but that wouldn't do anything to help that black painted line now.

Elizabeth put her hand on Jake's arm to caution him or he would have started to demand some explanation of how anyone could have let this happen. A wave of muffled voices greeted them as they walked up the aisle. Jake wasn't feeling too kindly toward his neighbors, but he tried not to show it. He even nodded to a few of the men; they didn't bother to nod back. Then he ushered Elizabeth and Spotted Fawn to a bench near the front on the Dry Creek side. He heard Higgins and Wells slip in behind him.

At least, Jake thought to himself, he knew who his friends in this town were. He looked across the aisle. Most of the men over there were merchants, except for Mr. Walls, the banker. All of them wore suits, though, even the barber who'd cut Higgins's hair. Jake hadn't really noticed before that none of the rougher element in town came to church. There should be some down-on-their luck miners somewhere. And the man who ran the livery stable. He knew dozens of Psalms by heart and was always quoting them. Where was he?

There was some rustling of skirts and Jake turned around to see Annabelle join Higgins and Wells on their bench.

There was more talking on the other side of the aisle.

Jake smiled at his friends. "Thanks for joining us."

"No need to thank me and Wells," Higgins said. "We both live on the creek, too. It's our home as much as it is yours."

Wells nodded.

Jake looked over at Annabelle. The store clerk's color was high.

"You live in town," Jake said to her softly. "You don't have to do this. I know you don't like trouble."

"Injustice is what I don't like."

Jake smiled. "I guess that means we're all forgiven?"

Annabelle nodded. "Mr. Higgins tells me he's giving up wolfing and I'm not one to hold a person's past against them once they've turned over a new leaf. Besides, if I can stand up for a wolf, I can certainly stand up for a little girl."

Jake turned to Higgins. "You've given up wolfing?"

Higgins cleared his throat uncomfortably. "Now that I'm getting some learning, I figure I can do something else."

Jake nodded. "Good. That's, well, good."

Times were definitely changing here in the Territory.

Elizabeth looked around her. She was stunned by Annabelle's decision to sit with Higgins. The woman was still wearing her mourning black. Her husband hadn't been dead for all that long. The other woman didn't look guilty about it, either. Of course, sitting with a man wasn't the same as marrying one as Elizabeth had done. And Annabelle's husband had been gone for a couple of months instead of a couple of weeks. No, Elizabeth decided, it wasn't the same at all.

Just then a man stood up on the other side of the room. The man was well-past fifty, bald and he wore a vest that stretched over his large stomach so tightly that the buttons were in danger of coming loose. The man's suit was gray and Elizabeth watched in fascination as he pointed a finger across the room. "Annabelle Bliss, I believe you're sitting in the wrong place."

Oh, dear. Elizabeth saw Annabelle press her hands together until the knuckles were white. There was still a pale strip on her finger where she'd taken off her wedding ring.

Annabelle whispered. "That's my boss. Mr. Broadman. He's the manager of the mercantile."

"Maybe you should go over," Elizabeth whispered back. She didn't want Annabelle to lose her job over this. After all, the other woman didn't have a husband to support her now so she needed that income to take care of herself and her son.

Annabelle just shook her head, took a deep breath and then stood up. "You know I can't abide injustice, Mr. Broadman. If you want to fire me over that, then you're welcome to do it right now. Just remember, I'm a good employee and you—you won't have anyone to open the store tomorrow if I'm not working."

Elizabeth decided Annabelle was the bravest woman in the room. She stood there in her black wool dress, the material so heavy that it fell limp from the waist. The dye in the cloth was uneven and there was no sheen to the black like most mourning dresses would have. She must have made the dress hurriedly from what material she could find at the time. There wasn't even a touch of lace anywhere to relieve the somber lines of it. And yet Annabelle's shoulders were straight and her eyes challenging, even if her breaths were quick and shallow.

A brown-suited man stood up on the other side of the aisle. "If you want to talk injustice, you need to talk to my sister. She lost her husband to them Indians." He pointed to Spotted Fawn. "And my sister isn't the only one to lose a loved one to the savages. Decent folks shouldn't have to be reminded of that sadness when they sit down in church."

"These are only two little girls," Annabelle shot back. "And one's a baby. They haven't done anything to anybody."

A woman in a feathered hat stood up on the other side. "Haven't done anything! That one there almost scared my little Susan to death, carrying on like she did behind the school. Giving some wild war cry and waving that piece of branch around. It's heathen ways is what it is—heathen, I tell you."

Just then there was a loud bang from the doorway.

"Enough!" Reverend Olson roared. He stood in the open doorway, with the gray overcast sky behind him and his black coat jacket moving slightly from the breeze coming through the door. "Is this any way for the children of God to act? And on the day of the Lord! You should be ashamed."

Everyone grew silent, even the children. Elizabeth looked at Jake sitting next to her. He certainly seemed relaxed in the midst of all of this shouting. Didn't he know fistfights could break out at any minute? Matthew would have left the room by now, or crawled under the bench.

Elizabeth gasped. She was horrified at her thoughts. Men were brave in different ways. She shouldn't compare one to the other. She was being disloyal and it was shameful. She needed a new dress. A nice black dress would do, something like the one Annabelle wore. The dead deserved some respect and she intended for Matthew to get what he was due. A person shouldn't just slip out of this life without someone grieving for him.

She moved a little farther away from Jake, just in case anyone was paying attention to how close she was sitting, which she could see no one was.

If Jake hadn't felt Elizabeth move a little farther down the bench, he would have clapped his hands after the reverend's speech. He didn't want to embarrass his wife with his actions, though. Not that everyone else wasn't staring at the minister just as much as Jake was. Even Spotted Fawn was caught up in it. Reverend Olson took his time looking over the crude line that had been painted down the middle of the room and the markings on the wall telling people where to sit.

"I want to talk to whoever did this after the service," the minister said. "In the meantime, I want everyone to know it will not be tolerated, especially not in the house of the Lord. Now, I'm going to ask everyone to get up and change the place where they are sitting. And I expect a goodly number of people to be on both sides of that line when we're finished, just like it used to be."

No one moved.

"You can't tell us where to sit," a woman's voice called out from the Miles City side.

The room was silent for a moment. Jake thought he recognized the voice and he was right. It was Mrs. Barker who stood up and adjusted her hat.

The reverend looked over the people again before finally saying, "If you're not willing to sit with your neighbors, no matter what the color of their skin, I'm going to ask you to leave the house of the Lord today."

Jake heard a series of gasps from men and women on both sides of the aisle.

"You can't ask us to leave church," Mrs. Barker finally said. "This is—well, it's *church*."

Reverend Olson smiled a little sadly. "I'm not asking you to leave. I'm asking you to stay in the grace of God and in good fellowship with your neighbors."

"I've never heard of such a thing," Mrs. Barker protested as she stepped out into the aisle. "This is our church. It belongs to this town."

"It's God's church," the minister replied. "It belongs to Him."

"Well, God's church will be empty then," Mrs. Barker said indignantly as she walked down the aisle to where the reverend stood. "You can't have a church with no people, remember that. And don't come complaining to me when the parents vote not to pay you for your work at the school, either."

Mrs. Barker turned to those still sitting on the benches and pointed her finger at them. "The rest of you, if you care about the future of this town, you'll get up and follow me out of here right now. We can't have Indians walking around like they belong here. If the railroad people see that, they'll never make us a stop. They're looking for civilized towns where their passengers will feel safe. No one feels safe with Indians sitting right next to them. Besides, it just isn't right."

With those words, Mrs. Barker walked straight out of the church. A flash of lightning streaked across the gray sky that showed through the open door, but no one paid it much attention, not even when the thunderclap followed. It only took a few minutes for most of the rest of the people to follow her out. Some of them stopped to murmur a few words to the reverend on their way, but none of them turned back to sit down again.

"Poor fools," Jake muttered to himself as the last Miles City person closed the door on their way out of the building.

Jake looked around and counted a total of nine people still inside. The reverend, himself, Elizabeth, Spotted Fawn, the baby, Annabelle, Higgins, Wells and Virginia Parker. The young woman surprised him. She was sitting in the back on the Dry Creek side, looking unsure of herself. Jake started to say something to her when the door opened again.

Annabelle's son, Tommy, walked in. The boy's hair was wild and his shirt had come untucked from his pants. Jake didn't know where the boy had been, but he could see his eyes grow wide as he walked down the aisle and looked around.

Jake was prepared for a question about where the

people had gone, but the first thing the boy said was, "Do I smell doughnuts?"

Jake grinned. At least some things never changed. "You sure do. And we have plenty to share, too." Jake looked up at the minister. "After the service, that is."

The Reverend Olson walked forward, too. He looked tired. "I think we have a few minutes for the boy to eat a doughnut before we begin the service. I wouldn't mind sitting a bit myself and having one, either. My wife wasn't feeling good so she didn't come this morning."

"Come, sit with us," Elizabeth spoke as she stood up and then looked at the girl next to her. "Spotted Fawn, can you help me pass out some of our doughnuts?" Elizabeth glanced back at the reverend. "You're sure there's time?"

He looked to the back of the room and addressed Virginia. "Does that work with your solo?"

"I'll be ready to sing whenever you want me to," the young woman said from where she sat. "Any time is fine."

Jake thought Virginia still looked a little unsure of herself, sitting alone in the back. He supposed she hadn't trusted her welcome enough to sit with the people of Miles City, not now that she was playing piano in that saloon of Colter's.

He nodded and smiled. She was welcome to sit with them—that much was for sure.

"I always look forward to your singing," the reverend said as he sat down on one of the benches. "You've got a lovely voice."

Jake was glad Elizabeth wasn't as fragile as

Virginia. Once Elizabeth had gotten past her determination to meet the angels right away, she'd always seemed to have her feet planted squarely on this earth. He appreciated that.

"Can I go get my friend?" Tommy asked after he'd taken a bite of his doughnut. "He won't want to miss out on this."

The reverend nodded. "Just get him back here quickly."

The boy started running down the aisle.

"Tommy!" his mother scolded him. "No running in church."

By then the boy was already outside. Annabelle turned to the reverend, "I'm sorry about that. I try to teach him better, but…without a father, I—"

Jake noticed Higgins go red in the face. No one else seemed to see it, though.

"After what this church has seen today, a boy running in the aisles is refreshing," the reverend said as he held up a half-eaten doughnut. "These are wonderful, by the way."

"They were going to be our peace offering," Elizabeth said as she quietly asked Spotted Fawn to pass the basket back to the man. "We thought maybe people would…" Her voice trailed off. "Well, I guess it didn't work."

Reverend Olson shook his head. "Now, we don't know that. It's still an act of faith. Sometimes faith takes time."

Just then Tommy burst back into the church. "They're coming."

"Who's coming?" his mother asked as she stood up, looking a little alarmed.

Tommy just turned to grin. He still had sugar on his

face. "I told them there were doughnuts and that Miss Virginia was going to sing. They like to hear her sing."

Jake's heart lifted when he saw who was coming through the door. The first man had the look of a hard-luck miner. The second was a soldier from the fort. The third was a drifter and the fourth looked like a trapper. None of them wore suits and they all needed a shave. But, they all stepped into the room with reverence, taking off what hats they had on their heads.

The last two through the door were Colter and the boy, Danny. Apparently, the boy had been released from jail. His light brown hair was newly cut and the wool pants on his lanky frame looked clean. Colter still had a hold on his collar, as though he didn't quite trust the boy yet.

Jake didn't blame him. The boy looked a little older than Spotted Fawn and full of vinegar. Colter appeared as bewildered about parenthood as Jake felt. Maybe more.

"Welcome," Jake said.

"Come have a doughnut—or two," Elizabeth said as she moved so Spotted Fawn could get to the aisle to pass the basket.

Jake watched over Elizabeth and Spotted Fawn until they had given out all of the doughnuts and grains of sugar was all that was left at the bottom of the basket. But by then, there were a good forty people in the church and none of them cared which side of the room they sat on.

When Elizabeth settled in next to him, Jake was content. Now that the folks who worried about appearances were gone, he could relax. It seemed the most natural thing in the world to put his hand over Elizabeth's hand as it lay on her lap. He snuggled the hand a little closer to him and she didn't object. He decided she was beginning to accept him as her husband and it made him feel good inside. He'd never expected being married would feel like this—as if the world was a better place just because someone else was in it.

Chapter Ten

Elizabeth felt the heat rush to her face. She supposed Annabelle meant well with her comments, but Elizabeth felt strange talking about Jake. So she bent her head to concentrate on the scrub brush she had in her hand. The church service was over and the women were all down on their knees trying to get rid of that black line while the men were out cutting firewood for the upcoming school week. The reverend had started to feel unwell and he was home now, hopefully eating some of the soup Annabelle had sent over for him and his wife.

"Well, anyway, I thought it was sweet," Annabelle finished up her thought as she leaned back. "The way your husband was holding your hand in church."

Elizabeth suddenly realized that Annabelle had been saying the word *husband* for the past ten minutes and the only face that had come into her mind had been Jake's.

"My husband's dead," she said in a twist of guilt.

"Oh," Annabelle said in surprise.

"Oh," Virginia echoed. Her blue eyes were wide with confusion, but she didn't say anything.

"Besides, it was chilly," Elizabeth finally added as she leaned into her scrubbing.

The women were silent after that.

Annabelle had lent both Elizabeth and Virginia old dresses to wear while they cleaned. The dresses hung a little loose on both Elizabeth and Virginia so they'd tied them tight with the strings of the aprons she'd also given them. They'd started by washing the mud off the entire floor so by now they were wet and dirty as they worked on the black line.

Spotted Fawn sat in the back of the room, playing with the baby.

Elizabeth didn't want either woman to think she was unfriendly. She paused in her scrubbing and leaned back to wipe her forehead.

"Have you noticed this isn't milk paint?" Elizabeth finally asked. That seemed like a safe topic. "I wish it was—it'd be easier to get off."

Milk paint was what poor people generally used. Elizabeth hadn't stirred up any for a few years, but she knew how to search out the right clays to give the mixture color. But she doubted many people here still made the lime and milk paint. It was too messy. And, like dyeing one's own cloth, it was going out of fashion.

"I suppose everyone buys that new oil paint now," Elizabeth continued. "I miss the colors of the milk paint, though. It makes such lovely soft, rich colors."

"I know what you mean," Annabelle said. She tucked

a few strands of her hair back into place. "We have some of that oil paint at the store, of course, but it's not the same. I forgot you'd mentioned you made your own colors. With that and the dyeing both. I've never done that."

"You do your own dyeing?" Virginia asked.

Elizabeth nodded. "I even made my own Turkish red calico last year. Oil-boiled, of course, and with wax for the pattern on the cloth. That was just extra, though. What I wanted most was to dye enough yarn for a small blanket."

"Really?" Virginia said. "I was thinking I might try to dye some of my old dresses." She flushed. "Nothing as complicated as an oil-boiled dye, of course. They're just getting faded and—well, I can't…"

The young woman let her voice trail off.

"No need to be shy about money with us," Annabelle said as she put her brush back in the rinse water. "Both of us are widows. We understand it's not easy for a woman to make her way without a man."

"That's true," Elizabeth added.

"I don't know what I would have done when my brother died if I hadn't gotten that job at Colter's saloon." Virginia wiped her reddened hands on her apron. "I wrote to my other brother, but I don't really know where he is. He hasn't written in years. And I couldn't stay at the fort. I'd applied everywhere else for a job and didn't find anything except with Colter."

"Well, I hear the man runs an honest place," Elizabeth said. Jake had told her that much.

"The men there respect him."

"Well, I'm glad he has the good sense to send you

home before dark. That's all I've got to say," Annabelle declared.

Elizabeth noticed the light in Virginia's eyes when they talked about the saloon owner. She wondered if the young woman had any idea that she was in love with the man. It was too bad, really, Elizabeth thought. She didn't suppose there was much to recommend a marriage between the two. Not even the way they looked together.

Virginia looked like a seashell, all white and pink and shiny clean. Colter was dark and lean. Elizabeth supposed he was handsome enough, but he reminded her more of a stormy day than a sunny one.

"I was pleased to see him come to church this morning." Elizabeth thought she should say what positive things she could about the man. Everyone deserved a chance. "And he brought the young boy with him—Danny."

Virginia nodded. "He keeps telling Danny to improve himself so he doesn't get sent back to that jail. That's why he brought him, I'm sure." She looked at Annabelle. "I'm glad Danny has made friends with your Thomas."

"If he wants to improve himself, Danny should be going to school, too." Annabelle put her brush down. "I know he doesn't, but Tommy must know him from somewhere and—" She stood up suddenly and put her hand to her heart. "Don't tell me Danny's been hanging around that—that place!"

"No, no," Virginia reassured her. "Colter doesn't let boys near the saloon. Well, except for Danny and he's in the back room washing dishes. I think the boys met at the sheriff's when Danny was in jail. The sheriff let them play checkers through the bars."

"In the *jail*. My baby's been going to the jail!" Annabelle walked over and sat down on the nearest bench. "I'm sorry. I just had no idea it would be so hard to raise a boy without a man to help. And me working all day."

"Higgins might help you out," Elizabeth said, a slight smile on her face.

"Why I'd never—" Annabelle started and then looked at Elizabeth. "No fair. I never said I was interested in Mr. Higgins. He's just a—a friend."

Elizabeth grinned. "I know."

Annabelle looked at her and started to smile back. "Okay, no more encouraging remarks for you, either. Although I am anxious to know how you and Jake are doing. I mean, I hope it's okay. I feel guilty for trying to talk you out of it earlier."

"You were trying to be helpful," Elizabeth said. She felt bad now for being so short with the woman earlier. If she'd known it was guilt that was prompting her comments, she would have assured her that things were fine.

"Like we all know, it's just hard for a woman alone," Annabelle said. "I was worried about you."

"I appreciate that," Elizabeth said. "But you can ease your mind. Jake is a perfect gentleman."

"I wish Colter were a perfect gentleman," Virginia said, and then blushed. "I mean, he doesn't even know I'm there and I'm playing the piano so everybody should know I'm there. Why I've played 'Amazing

Grace' several times and he hasn't even moved. Some of those men in there have wept when I've played that song, especially when I sing it, too. And he doesn't even blink an eye."

The young woman bristled with such indignation that her smooth blond bun quivered slightly on the back of her neck.

"I think he was half-asleep," she continued. This time her voice wavered a little.

"Well, he might not know the song," Annabelle said kindly. "He's wearing a suit now, but I'd guess Colter had a rough life before he got that saloon of his. He's probably not too familiar with hymns."

"I guess," the younger woman said and then sighed. "I just don't understand men."

"If it's any consolation, neither do I, dear, neither do I," Annabelle said. "And I've been married twice before."

"Twice?" Elizabeth asked.

Annabelle nodded. "I've buried two husbands. Tommy's dad and then my last husband."

"I'm sorry," Elizabeth murmured. It didn't seem fair that a woman should have to bear that grief twice. And Annabelle was only ten or so years older than she was.

The three women sat and looked at each other for a minute or so. Elizabeth thought it was a nice silence. It occurred to her that she was actually making some new friends. She wasn't going to want to leave this place in the spring.

"I could help you if you want to dye some things," Elizabeth said as she turned to Virginia and then looked back at Annabelle. "And you probably have some things of Thomas's that you'd like dyed."

Both women nodded.

"I'd like that," Virginia added.

"Could we do it before Christmas?" Annabelle asked.

"I don't see why not," Elizabeth declared. She had presents to make, as well. "Although we still need to figure out what to do here."

"I suppose we could paint the whole floor black," Annabelle said dubiously. "But we only have one can of black paint in the store right now and that wouldn't be enough. Besides, even if we could get it covered, it wouldn't be dry before school tomorrow. Not with the amount of paint we'd need to use."

"I have the afternoon off," Virginia offered, "but if the paint won't dry…"

"We don't need to paint the whole floor," Elizabeth said. "I have an idea."

Jake shifted the trunk of the tree he was carrying over his shoulder. He and the other men had walked toward the fort far enough to come to the wooded area that the soldiers used when they needed firewood. Higgins, Wells and Colter each had an old cottonwood on their shoulders, too. They'd only bothered to strip the bigger limbs off the trees and one of the remaining smaller branches of his tree was scratching Jake on the back of his neck.

"Explain to me again why these trees will burn so slow the reverend will hardly ever need to feed the fire,"

Jake said as he stopped to set his tree down so he could break off the offending branch. Then he turned to the men behind him. "You're the one who said it, Higgins."

"Well, I didn't say no one would ever need to feed the fire," Higgins objected as he let his own tree slide to the ground. "I just said it should burn longer because these pieces will be so thick."

"They're thick all right," Wells said as he let his own tree fall to the ground. "And heavy."

Jake rubbed the back of his neck. He wouldn't have those tree scratches if he'd kept all his hair. Oh, well. "I'm not sure anyone will show up for school Monday anyway so it might not even be worth it to have a fire."

Jake knew all of those responsible citizens filing out of church this morning were bound to make some changes. He figured school is where they'd start.

"Let me know if they don't come." Colter let down his own burden. "I'll send Danny over if I know—" The man broke off.

"I'm sure there's room for Danny even if everyone else is there," Jake said as he sat down on his tree just as Higgins and Wells had done with theirs. "The reverend invites all of the children to school."

Colter turned around. "I haven't sent the boy before because I was worried the kids would make fun of him. His mother used to work in one of the other saloons, you know."

"And his father?" Jake asked.

Colter snorted. "See, that's the kind of thing he'd face. Some folks assume I'm his father—poor kid—but

I only met his mother a couple of years ago. And then only to say hello. She died soon after and, well, there was no place for the boy to go so I figured working in a saloon was better than starving to death."

"Don't worry about him," Jake said. "Higgins will be there so he'll see that things go okay for him."

Colter looked over at Higgins in surprise. "You're teaching school?"

"Not teaching. Going," Higgins said proudly. "I aim to learn to read."

"A man doesn't need to know how to read," Wells protested. "Knowing how to read won't get these logs to the school any faster, now will it?"

"Well, maybe not," Jake said as he stretched out his legs. "But it would be mighty nice to sit by the fire that comes from these logs and read a book some evening."

"Women like that, don't they?" Colter asked. "Reading by the firelight?"

Jake nodded. "Most women, I'd say. They think it's romantic."

Jake was reminding himself to buy a book of poetry for Elizabeth. He kept remembering that the soldier at the fort had written his own poem for Elizabeth, but Jake didn't know if he could do that. A nice leather-backed book of poems should convey his feelings just as well.

Then Jake realized it was someone else who had thought of the romance of words first and he looked at the saloon keeper more closely. "You got some particular woman in mind for your firelight reading?"

Colter shrugged. "Maybe."

Jake frowned. He shifted his weight on the tree in case he had to stand. "Well, I hope it's not Virginia Parker. She's a decent woman and—"

"Don't you think I don't know that?" Colter interrupted in disgust. "Why do you think I make her leave my saloon before my business even starts?"

"I don't know. I never did understand why you hired her in the first place. The only kind of piano playing she can do is hymns."

"I know. She's chased away most of my customers. And the ones who haven't gone have either sworn off their whiskey or they sit there, sobbing into their drinks and talking to their dead mothers. Even my bartender is threatening to quit. He says it's depressing to watch grown men behave that way."

"Well, there must be some other job for her in a town the size of Miles City."

"She's already got a job," Colter said as he stood up. "At my place."

So that's the way it was, Jake thought as he stood, as well. "A woman like that deserves a home and marriage and—"

"I know, I know," Colter said as he walked ahead a bit and kicked a couple of rocks out of the way. Jake thought the man did it with more force than necessary, but he supposed it was just as well. It was a hard thing when a man set his eyes on a woman who was out of his reach.

"Well, let's get started again," Jake said as Higgins and Wells both stood up. "We've got to get these trees back to the school so we can take an ax to them."

"Isn't this Sunday?" Higgins grumbled as he lifted his tree. "It's supposed to be a day of rest."

"Well, this Sunday isn't," Jake answered as he lifted his, too. He hoped the women were having an easier afternoon than the men were. "Whose idea was this to bring in these trees anyway?"

No one owned up to it.

By the time the men carried their old trees into the school yard, the afternoon was starting to fade. They pulled the trees around to the back of the schoolhouse to where the woodpile usually was.

"Looks like the reverend has enough wood to keep the fire going for most of a day," Jake said. "Maybe I'll just wait until tomorrow to come around and chop this log up for him."

It would give him a chance to check on the students, Jake thought. Even Elizabeth couldn't accuse him of not being tactful if he was chopping wood while he was looking around.

"I can come over in the afternoon to help, too. There isn't anything happening at my place anyway," Colter offered. "Besides, well, I'd just feel better keeping an eye on things."

Jake looked at the man. "You know something or is it just a hunch?"

Colter shrugged. "A little of both. Danny said he thought he overheard some of the boys talking about doing something Monday."

"Well, why didn't you say anything before?"

"I'm saying it now," Colter protested. "Besides, he

wasn't sure. He was slipping around to enter the saloon by the back door when he saw a couple of the older boys sitting there. They stopped talking while he walked by, but he thought he heard them say something about school or Sam Lee's laundry. He wasn't sure which."

"I can't imagine what they'd want with Sam Lee. I don't see those boys being overly concerned about clean clothes."

"Boys sometimes just talk big," Higgins said. "Maybe those boys didn't mean anything."

Colter nodded. "That's one of the reasons I didn't say anything earlier."

"And the other reason?" Jake asked.

Colter looked him in the eye. "I wasn't sure anyone would believe Danny anyway. Not after him stealing that watch."

"Does the boy make a habit of lying?" Jake asked.

"I've never known him to. Boys are hard to know sometimes, though. I get the feeling he's at one of those places in his life where he could go either way."

"Well, the boy's had a hard life," Higgins said.

Colter nodded. "I'm the closest thing he has to a parent and I don't really know what to do for him."

"You feed him, clothe him—you brought him to church," Jake said. "That's a good start."

"Well, I only got him to come to church because he knew Virginia was going to sing. He worships that woman. Says he's going to marry her when he grows up."

"Oh," Jake said in surprise and then he thought about it a minute. "Oh."

"I know." Colter said wryly. "Any other competition I wouldn't mind."

"Well, what'd the boy say he heard?" Higgins asked impatiently. "That's the important thing."

"He just said they were talking about showing them Indian lovers a thing or two." Colter looked chagrined. "Sorry. Those aren't my words. Danny also said they were going to pound the mountain man. I wondered how they could describe Sam Lee that way, but now that I know Higgins is going to school, I figure they must mean him."

"Well, just let them try!" Higgins bellowed.

"Keep your voice down," Jake said with a look at the schoolhouse. "We don't want to get the women all worried."

The men were silent for a bit. They were at the back of the schoolhouse so Jake listened for the sound of the front door opening. He didn't hear anything.

"I guess we might as well see how the women are doing anyway," Jake said.

"I doubt they could get that paint off with those brushes of theirs. I don't think it can be done," Colter said.

Jake was of the same opinion, but he wasn't about to say anything. He'd come to realize that women had their own way of solving problems and he wasn't betting against them. Not anymore. Especially not when Elizabeth was involved.

Chapter Eleven

Jake walked into the schoolhouse and stopped. If it wasn't for some old cards his mother had kept in a box by her bed, he wouldn't recognize what he saw. It was Christmas. Yellow stars were painted on the black line in the middle of the floor and red-berried holly twined around them both. The women had their backs to him and hadn't heard him come inside. They were standing at the front of the room painting Merry Christmas on the Dry Creek side of the wall. There were even red-painted bells ringing over the words and more stars falling everywhere.

"You've been busy," Jake said as the other men crowded into the room behind him. He glanced over and saw his nieces were curled up together, sleeping on a blanket in a corner of the room.

"Don't walk on the line," Elizabeth said as she turned around. "It's not dry yet."

Jake grinned. His beautiful wife had a dab of yellow

on her cheek and a streak of red on the back of her hand. And she looked happy. "We'll be careful."

"I guess you decided not to scrub it all away," Colter said as he carefully walked closer to the line and looked down at all of the painted stars and berries.

Jake wondered if the other man recognized what he saw.

"Christmas," Jake said quietly and the other man nodded.

"We came up with a different plan." Virginia turned around and smiled at Colter. Well, actually, she beamed at the man. Jake was surprised Colter managed to sit down on one of the benches before his legs gave out. Jake was only getting the reflection of the look and it knocked him back a little, too.

It was hard to tell if Virginia was beaming because of the man or because of her excitement over what she was doing. She held a paintbrush that had been dipped in yellow paint and she waved it around freely as she spoke.

"It was really Elizabeth's idea but everyone, even the reverend, thought it was wonderful," Virginia continued, with such enthusiasm a man could only conclude it was the painting that was the cause of her exuberance at the moment.

Jake saw Colter's jaw tighten a little and he almost felt sorry for the man. It must be a disappointment to lose out to a holiday the man probably didn't even celebrate.

"All kids love Christmas," Elizabeth explained as she carefully put her paintbrush down in an empty tin can. "So we decided to remind everyone that the season of goodwill is coming soon. There'll be time enough to paint over the whole floor after Christmas. And the front wall, too."

The men were silent for a moment, letting everything sink in.

"Well, the stars are real nice," Jake said. "I'm partial to them myself."

He always had liked reading about how the star guided the wise men on their trip. He could relate to men like that. Not to the value of their gifts, of course, but he knew many men who traveled in search of something they weren't sure they'd find.

Men like Higgins, for instance. Jake noticed that the man had quietly made his way up to the wall where Annabelle was painting a sprig of holly.

His partner, Wells, though, appeared to be looking for treasure of a different sort. He eyed the empty basket that Spotted Fawn had carried around this morning. "I don't suppose you'll be making any more of those doughnuts? To celebrate the goodwill and all."

"I plan to make another batch for the children," Elizabeth said. "Most of them didn't get any this morning. And we want to have lots of good things for Christmas."

"Could there be pies, too?" Wells asked. "My mother used to make the best pecan pies for Christmas."

Jake had never heard the man mention a longing for pie before. Or a mother, either.

"Pies, too," Elizabeth agreed. "I even have some pecans in a box just waiting to be used."

The years rolled away and Jake remembered his

mother trying to make a pie once. He'd picked some berries for her; he'd long since forgotten what kind they were. But his mother had spent the morning making a crust and finally had slipped the pie into the oven. The heat had been too hot, or the plate too full, because the berries juiced up and spilled over and onto the bottom of the stove. It had taken the rest of the day to get the smoke out of the cabin and his mother had declared the pie too ruined to eat. She'd never tried to make another one.

Jake brought himself back to the present. One thing he knew was that Elizabeth wouldn't have given up after one try.

"We talked to Reverend Olson," Elizabeth was saying, her voice quietly excited. "And we're going to work with the students to put on a Christmas pageant."

"For the whole town," Virginia added as she spread her arms out and twirled around. "Isn't that wonderful? The children are going to be angels. And sing."

Jake exchanged a worried look with Colter and then asked. "All of the children?"

"Of course," said Virginia.

"I'm not sure the older boys will—" Colter began until Virginia started to look disappointed. "I mean, they may need to have special costumes. The little children can wear a man's shirt or something, but—"

"We've got the costumes all planned out," Virginia said as she brightened again. "Elizabeth said we can use the old union suits that are packed away in the things from her wagon. We can put something with them if we need to make them whiter. Or dye them if we want, although then I'm not sure she'll be able to sell them afterward. Anyway, they'll be big enough to fit the boys so they're perfect. In fact, we'll need to cut them down for the younger children." Virginia stopped to take a breath.

She looked right at Colter.

"I'm sure they'll be grateful for the ah—" Colter cleared his throat "—for the opportunity to perform."

"And it's not like they'll have wings or anything," Jake added hopefully. Someone needed to say something and it was obvious Colter wasn't able to get the words out. If there were no wings, the boys might be able to tell themselves they were trees or rocks or something.

"Wings!" Virginia exclaimed. "Of course, we'll need to make wings."

Jake had a sinking feeling. "What time are you planning to announce this to the kids?"

"Tomorrow morning just after they finish working their sums. About ten o'clock." Elizabeth walked over and stood beside Virginia. "We wanted to wait until they finished so the excitement wouldn't distract them from it."

Jake nodded. He looked over at Colter and the other man dipped his head in answer. They'd both be outside the schoolhouse cutting wood about then. They knew those boys wouldn't agree to wear wings without a fight. Fortunately, the women hadn't mentioned halos yet. Jake knew he wasn't going to even say a word about that.

"I don't suppose some of the boys could be innkeepers or something?" Jake asked. He guessed they'd rather sweep the floor than flap their wings with the girls, but he wasn't too sure. "Or maybe shepherds? Shepherds would be okay."

It wouldn't be the cowboys these boys dreamed of becoming, but at least being a shepherd was a man's job and they would be proud to do it.

"Well, we should have a Joseph, I suppose." Elizabeth bit her lip in thought. "And a Mary and the Baby Jesus."

"Mary and Joseph could be adults." Annabelle turned around finally to join the conversation. "It is supposed to be a pageant for the whole community. Adults should do their part."

Jake wondered what Mrs. Barker's Civic Improvement League would think of the pageant. On this issue he might even agree with her. He sympathized with any boy that had to wear a halo or wings or pretend to be married to someone he probably didn't like.

But, even if they had Mrs. Barker behind them, these boys would have a hard time going against Christmas. Not because they cared whether they were holy or not. No, it would just eventually become clear that, if there was no Christmas, there'd be no doughnuts. He was sure rumors of those doughnuts had reached all the boys in town by now.

Elizabeth felt tired and happy as she rode home in the wagon with Jake and the girls. She had the baby in her arms and Spotted Fawn was sitting on the seat between her and Jake. It made Elizabeth feel as though they were a real family, sitting together after all they'd been through that day.

There was little more than a rut for the wagon wheels to follow as they drove home. After the overcast skies that morning, the afternoon sun had come out and dried the dirt so the wheels turned smoothly.

"I'm glad it's not raining still," Elizabeth said. "It's going to take most of the night for that paint to dry as it is. If it rained, I don't know if the floor would be ready for school in the morning."

"It wouldn't be such a bad thing if school couldn't meet for a day or two." Jake pulled on the reins slightly to signal the horses to make a wide turn. They were almost to the last small rise before they dipped down and could see the first signs of home.

"Oh, but the children have to go to school."

"I know, but a day or two wouldn't matter much."

They were both silent for a bit.

"Do you think we did the right thing?" Elizabeth finally asked. "Leaving the Miles City side of the room bare for the others to paint? We didn't want to look like we were taking over everything. I mean—maybe they don't want to wish anyone Merry Christmas."

"It wouldn't be very neighborly not to say Merry Christmas."

Elizabeth nodded. She supposed so. It bothered her that, even though they had painted things over that line on the floor, the line was still there in her mind. It was now Miles City and Dry Creek; everyone made the distinction. Annabelle, Jake, Higgins, even Wells. When they had left for church this morning, they were one community and now, only eight hours later, they were two.

Elizabeth wondered if that was progress or not. She supposed it was too early to judge that really. So far, Dry Creek didn't have much to recommend it. There was no good road to where Jake had his cabin. No school. No hotel. Nothing but a flat stretch of gray dirt with a few ripples in the landscape and those cottonwood trees. In time, though, things could change. Maybe a little community would grow here someday and have some of the same kind of heart the Dry Creek side of things had shown this morning.

But she doubted she would be around to see it. Even with all of the friendship she'd seen today, she didn't feel easy in her heart about staying here. She didn't know what she would do in the spring.

"We're home," Jake said softly and Elizabeth noticed that Spotted Fawn had gone to sleep next to her uncle. The baby was sleeping, too.

"It's been a long day," Elizabeth whispered back.

Jake bedded the horses down for the night and fed the other animals before he started toward the cabin for supper. It was dusk. He stopped a moment to look around his land. The cottonwood trees sheltered him from the east. The ravine that dipped down to the creek was close enough that hauling water was no problem. The emptiness that stretched in all directions made some people uneasy, but it gave him peace.

This was a good place to live. He would improve on it over the years, of course. Maybe he'd send a telegraph and order another load of lumber for when the Missouri river opened up again and the steamboats were able to make the trip up to Fort Benton. Whether or not Elizabeth stayed with them, the girls needed a better home. He might as well start on it this summer.

In the meantime, he reminded himself to buy more coal oil for the lamp. One nice thing about having a family was he was using the lamp more often in the evening. He felt satisfaction just walking to the house and seeing the warm glow coming from the windows. One day soon, he'd see about getting some new books, too.

The smell of fried onions greeted him when he stepped in the door. Two plates had been set on the table and Elizabeth was standing by the stove. She'd worn the dress she'd used for scrubbing the floor home, but had changed into one of her own dresses. It wasn't any newer than her scrubbing one, but it was clean and dry.

"Spotted Fawn already ate and went to bed," Elizabeth said. "And I fed the baby, so she's sleeping, too."

Jake glanced up to the loft and stepped closer to Elizabeth. He kept his voice low. "Did Spotted Fawn mention wanting to run away again?"

Elizabeth shook her head and whispered. "I think the promise of celebrating Christmas will keep her here for a while. She could barely keep her eyes open while she ate and she was still asking questions about it."

"She likes the story of it all. She used to sit and listen to the old people of her tribe tell stories for hours," Jake said before he turned to look at the stove. "That smells good."

"It's just fried potatoes and onions. Annabelle mentioned it to me. It's one of her son's favorites. She gave me a couple of onions from her root cellar. I'll have to plant some in my garden this year. She also gave me a recipe for elk stew and I gave her mine for stewed tomatoes."

Elizabeth took the frying pan off the stove and walked to the table. "I'm thinking I'll have some use for the elk one."

"I should go hunting soon." Jake turned toward the table, too. He had been pleased to see how much Elizabeth enjoyed the company of Annabelle and Virginia. His mother had always complained of her solitude. Maybe the territory had grown up enough in the years since then that a woman could find some social life even if it was only exchanging recipes and painting stars on the schoolhouse floor.

Elizabeth spooned the potatoes and onions onto their plates.

"I never knew you could do so many things," Jake said as he sat down. "Virginia said you even know how to make soap. And your own dyes. I didn't know ladies back East knew how to do any of those things."

Elizabeth set the spoon back in the pan. She supposed, at heart, all men were the same. "Not every woman can be a lady, you know. Not when it takes so much work to run a household."

Jake gave her a look of surprise.

Now, she'd done it, Elizabeth thought. "I'm sorry to be snappish. I just—I just—well, I guess I'm tired."

They were both seated at the table by now, but neither made any move to say a prayer so they could eat. Jake was looking at her as if he was expecting her to say more.

"Of course, you are," Jake finally said. "And this afternoon probably brought back lots of memories."

Now it was Elizabeth's turn to look at him. What did he mean?

"Of Christmas," he explained. "My mother always was a little sad when she looked through her Christmas things. Too many memories, I suppose, along with the trinkets and cards she'd kept from her childhood."

"I'm fine with Christmas," Elizabeth said and bowed her head. It was true; she always had been fine with Christmas as long as she didn't let herself dream about it being special.

Jake looked at her a moment and then bowed his head, too. "Thank you, Father, for this day. And for our neighbors. May you show us how to live peacefully together. And, thank you for this food Elizabeth has made for us. May You keep us in Your hands. Amen."

"Amen," Elizabeth echoed as she reached for her spoon.

"I suppose you have some Christmas things in your boxes," Jake said as he started to eat. "Things from your childhood."

"No."

Jake stopped eating and looked at Elizabeth. He knew how much his mother valued her Christmas things. They made her sad, but they had also made her happy reliving the memories. "I suppose your husband didn't think there was room for them in the wagon."

Jake never had liked Matthew. Which was a terrible thing to say about a man who was dead in the ground, but there it was.

"I didn't have anything to bring," Elizabeth said. "I mean—I do have some yarn I dyed bright red so I could make Rose a blanket for her first Christmas present, but that's all."

"But you must have memories, too." Jake persisted. Even he had some memories of holidays when his father had whittled him a horse or a grizzly and his mother had given him hard candy she'd hoarded from the last time his father had been to a trading post.

Elizabeth was looking down at her plate as though like she'd just as soon avoid this conversation. Maybe she didn't want to remember because she knew it wouldn't be the same this year.

"I'm sorry. I know memories can be best left alone," Jake finally said. "I don't mean to pry."

Elizabeth finally looked at him. "There's nothing to pry into. I didn't have time to celebrate Christmas as a child. There was too much to do getting everything ready for the family. I had to scrub all of the windows so someone could put pine boughs over them. I had to chop nuts and knead dough for the fruit buns people wanted. And then there were the pies and the puddings. I was usually allowed some time off after Christmas dinner was served, but I was so exhausted all I wanted to do was sleep."

"But surely your parents—"

"My parents were dead." Elizabeth had only taken a few bites of her fried potatoes, but she pushed her plate away.

"I'm sorry," Jake said as he pushed back his chair and stood up. "I didn't realize—"

"Of course not," Elizabeth said as she stood, as well. She gave a forced little smile. "And I can't say I never had anything of Christmas. When I was real little, the cooks almost always saved me something good to eat. If a gingerbread cookie was broken, it would be set aside for me. Sometimes I had an orange of my own to eat. And new shoes. One year, the family I was with got me new shoes for Christmas. That was in my agreement with them. I was to get a pair of shoes and a new dress for my work that year, so I would have gotten them anyway, but it was nice they did it on Christmas."

"How old were you when your parents died?"

Elizabeth shrugged. "I've tried to figure that out myself. I can't remember. There didn't seem to be any marking of the time. It feels like I was with them one week and the next I was working at my first house, expected to go on like it was just the passing of one week to the other."

"That must have been hard."

Jake decided that some days a man needed to hold his wife for his own comfort as much as hers. He held out his arms and Elizabeth walked into them. She was stiff as though she'd come to him reluctantly.

"Anything wrong?"

"I—I" Elizabeth stepped back from him and looked at his chin. She looked miserable, but determined at the same time.

"You can tell me," Jake said. "Whatever it is, it's okay."

She looked at him square this time. "I'm sorry, but I want to wear mourning for Matthew."

Jake tried to keep the flinch he felt inside from showing on his face. "But Matthew isn't your husband anymore."

"I know. It's just that it's like with my parents. Just because someone moves me to a different house, that doesn't mean I should erase all my memories of who I used to belong with."

"I'm sure no one meant for you to do that with your parents."

"Maybe not. But there was no room to grieve for them. No way to mark their passing. I don't want to do the same thing with Matthew. He was a good man. He deserves to have someone pay attention to his death."

Jake nodded. He might not like it, but he could almost understand it. "How can I help?"

"I'll need to have a black dress," Elizabeth said hesitantly. "Usually, I would dye some fabric, but with all we need to do to get ready for Christmas, I—"

"Buy what you need."

"I'm not asking you to buy me a dress. I have some red calico I'm pretty sure I can sell or trade for enough black cloth. This is something I need to do myself. All I really want is your blessing."

Jake looked at her for a full minute before he nodded.

"Thank you," Elizabeth said and then turned back to the stove. She felt more tired than she had when she was lying in her tent waiting to die. She had not realized when she agreed to Jake's suggestion that marrying him would be so hard for her. She hadn't given up her life with Matthew and Rose; it had been jerked away from her. She needed time to grieve before she could open her heart to a new family.

She heard the door close as Jake let himself out of the house.

Chapter Twelve

Jake had never expected to have his wife dress up like a widow, at least not while he was alive, but that's what was happening. It hadn't taken Elizabeth long to start looking for a black dress. He and Elizabeth had both come into town Monday morning to be sure that Spotted Fawn was at school on time. Even before school was scheduled to start, however, Elizabeth had walked into the mercantile with some brilliant red cloth and asked Annabelle to put it up for sale or trade so she could buy a black mourning dress.

"I'll walk Spotted Fawn to the school," Jake said when he heard Elizabeth ask her question. He wanted no part of that black dress. He had the baby with him and the fresh air would do them both good. He'd bring the baby back before long so she could take her morning nap at Annabelle's.

Annabelle watched Jake and Spotted Fawn leave the mercantile before she turned her attention back to

Elizabeth. "What are you doing? Jake's your husband. He's not dead."

"But my other husband is," Elizabeth protested. "I don't know how you do it. I can't just walk away from my old life. Everything's happening too fast."

Annabelle put her hand on Elizabeth's arm. "You poor thing. It has been fast. I keep forgetting that. It's just that you and Jake seem so right together."

"It was okay at first, I mean we only got married to take care of the baby, but—"

Annabelle smiled. "It's becoming real."

Elizabeth looked up at her new friend. "I just don't know anymore. If I'd been the one to die from the fever, I hope Matthew would grieve for me. At least for a little while. A person should leave a mark on someone's life when they leave this world."

"I remember feeling that way when Tommy's father died. I was alive and he was dead and there was no rhyme nor reason to it all. I was full up with guilt inside. Thought I should have done more for him when he'd been alive. Wished I had just one more minute with him to tell him how sorry I was for always fussing at him over his muddy boots."

Elizabeth nodded. "Matthew was terrible with his boots, too."

The women were silent for a bit.

"Well, if it's a mourning dress you want, you're welcome to have mine," Annabelle said. "The old thing itches and it's the ugliest thing around, but you're welcome to it. I can't wear it for work anyway and it seems foolish to wear it to church when I don't wear it for the rest of the week."

"You'd let me have your dress?" Nothing had ever sounded more comforting to Elizabeth than to wear her friend's mourning dress. "I'll trade you for it, of course. You can have the red calico if you want—to sell or use."

"I won't take anything for that old mourning dress. A friend of mine in Helena gave it to me so I didn't pay anything for it, anyway." Annabelle looked at the fabric Elizabeth held in her arms. "Is this the cloth you dyed yourself?"

Elizabeth nodded as she took a lingering look at it.

"You should keep it," Annabelle said. "You've put a lot of work into that cloth."

"I need to give up something that means something to me to get a mourning dress. It doesn't feel right not to have something taken away."

"Well, I'll keep it for you for a while, if that's what you want. We'll talk about what to do with it later." Annabelle reached out to touch the cloth. "It's so pretty. It gives the whole place a Christmas look."

"Thank you," Elizabeth said.

Annabelle nodded.

"Here, let me close the store for a minute while we go in the back and get the dress for you," Annabelle said as she reached under the counter and brought out a silver bell. "One of the nice things about this job is being able to slip back to our rooms when I need to."

"It is a good job for you," Elizabeth agreed as she

followed Annabelle to the back. "You're sure things are okay with Mr. Broadman? He's not still threatening to fire you, is he?"

Annabelle shook her head as she unlocked the door leading to her quarters. "He already stopped by. He's calmed down by now. He just gets riled up when Mrs. Barker claims someone needs to do something to be sure the railroad comes through here. I think he'd jump off a bridge if that woman told him it would bring the railroad. He always settles down later, though."

Annabelle opened the door to a small parlor.

"Well, she might be right in some of the things she says," Elizabeth said as they both walked into the room. "I don't know anything about what would make the railroad chose one place over another."

"I'm beginning to realize that we need to live in this town whether the railroad comes or not. We need to be a good town, no matter what comes."

The furniture in the parlor was well-worn, but sturdy. An ivory wallpaper covered the walls and light brown curtains hung over the windows.

Annabelle helped Elizabeth try on the mourning dress. It was a little loose on her, but they both decided it would do fine.

"It needs a good washing," Annabelle said.

Elizabeth nodded as she started to remove the dress.

"Just don't put it in water that's too hot," Annabelle added. "I made that mistake and the black color faded so bad it isn't worth much anymore."

Elizabeth examined the dress as she stood there in her

chemise and petticoats. "It looks like whoever dyed it didn't set it properly. It's easy to forget that the water needs to be boiling when you add the soda ash."

The bell rang out in the front of the store.

"Oh, I've got to go," Annabelle said. "Take your time. And I can't wait to hear how excited the kids are today when you and Virginia tell them about the pageant. I didn't tell Tommy so he can hear it with the others."

Elizabeth nodded as she finished putting her regular dress back on. She'd go over to the school and wait for the children to finish their sums. Virginia said she'd meet her there.

Jake felt the ax sink into the side of the log. He and Colter had a rhythm to their chopping even though they were both working on different logs. Jake found himself thinking about that dress his wife was wanting and he started bringing the ax down faster and with more force with every thought he had. Then he realized Colter was matching his pace.

"What's ailing you?" Jake stopped chopping to ask.

The other man might be a business owner, but he didn't lack staying power when it came to work. Colter had taken off his vest and rolled up his sleeves. His shirt was drenched in sweat. He stopped swinging his ax and put his arm up to wipe his forehead.

"Business," Colter said.

"Losing money, are you?"

"It's my employees if you must know. Someone's taking money from the till."

"Ahh."

"I think I know who it is, but—"

"I hope you don't think its Virginia Parker. She wouldn't take a dime that didn't belong to her."

"I know, I know. The woman's a saint. No, I think it's the guy tending bar. But—"

"But you don't know for sure."

"And it could be Danny."

"Ahh." Jake sympathized with the man. "I don't know what I'd do if Spotted Fawn started stealing things. Not that—I mean, the Sioux don't really see possessions like we do, but if she was taking money I'd need to put a stop to it somehow. It could be a problem."

Colter nodded. "I don't know what real parents do."

"You might ask Annabelle. Her son, Tommy, seems like he's turning out all right."

"I might do that. If I can think of a way to ask without sounding like I'm accusing anyone of anything. I don't want people to say I think Danny is thieving." Colter put his ax up to make another swing. "Folks get their minds around something like that and they don't let go even if it turns out not to be true."

Jake pulled his ax up, as well. He wasn't about to be outdone by a businessman.

It wasn't two minutes later before both men stopped chopping. They could see Elizabeth and Virginia walking down the street, getting ready to turn into the walk that went to the schoolhouse.

"Did you get a chance to tell them how few kids are in school today?" Colter asked.

Jake shook his head.

"Well, at least we don't have to worry about those boys today," Colter said. "I can't see why they'd want to make trouble in a classroom when they don't even need to go near the place."

"That makes sense." Not that it was good news when a man looked at the whole picture, but there was nothing to be done about it at the moment.

"In that case, maybe it wouldn't hurt to go in and hear what the ladies have to say," Colter said, trying to appear casual about it.

"They'd probably appreciate the company."

Jake heard the door to the schoolhouse open. He was looking at the back of the building, but that must be the women going inside.

Elizabeth stood in the open doorway. She took a deep breath as Virginia waited by her side. There were exactly five people in the schoolroom. The reverend, Spotted Fawn, Thomas, Danny and Mr. Higgins. Of those, Spotted Fawn was the only one who probably had any interest in being an angel in a Christmas pageant.

"I guess all of our painting didn't work," Elizabeth whispered to Virginia. "None of the kids from Miles City are here. And I know the reverend was going to ask Mrs. Barker over to see everything this morning."

The yellow stars and the trailing holly weren't as shiny today as they had been yesterday. Even with fires in both stoves, the room was chilly. Elizabeth supposed it was because the heat from all of the other children was missing. She even missed the musty smell of the damp wool scarves and mittens that were usually drying on a chair near the stoves.

"We can't force people to be nice to each other," Virginia said.

"That's what laws are for," Elizabeth said. "To keep people civilized."

"Well, we can't arrest people for not saying Merry Christmas to each other."

By now, Reverend Olson had looked up and seen them.

"Come on in, ladies," he said with a welcoming smile. "We're just finishing our sums."

Elizabeth nodded and she and Virginia stepped farther into the school room.

"The ladies have some exciting news for you," the reverend said, with as much enthusiasm as he would have used if the room had been filled with children.

"Well," Elizabeth began. "Miss Virginia and I are here to see if you'd like to put on a Christmas pageant. There would be lots of angels and Miss Virginia would lead them in singing songs and—"

A hand went up.

"Yes, Danny?"

"Can I be one of the singers with Miss Virginia?"

Elizabeth nodded. She felt much better now. If even Danny was glowing with excitement about their news, the others would soon realize how much fun it could be. "I think that can be arranged."

Jake and Colter opened the schoolhouse door and slipped into the last bench. Virginia was singing one of the songs the women planned to use in the pageant and her voice rose and dipped over everyone like a flock of songbirds coming home to rest. When Virginia had finished singing, Colter gave a deep sigh.

Jake knew it wasn't the music that moved the other man and he could have sighed right along with him. Neither one of them was doing very well with the women they wanted to impress.

Wham! Jake heard the sound of some kind of bullet right outside the schoolhouse. Then there was another one.

"Everyone down!" Jake ordered as he, Colter and Higgins fanned out and each slid toward one of the windows. Colter had his pistol drawn and Higgins had stopped to pick up a good-sized piece of firewood. Jake put his hand on the knife he had strapped around his thigh. His rifle was out by the woodpile behind the school.

Wham! There was an explosion on the other side of the schoolhouse.

Jake looked at Colter. "That doesn't sound like a bullet."

"It's firecrackers," Higgins said. "Made by Sam Lee, I expect."

Just then, Jake saw a flash of blue as a boy took off running.

"Elias Barker," Jake muttered. He should have known.

Higgins must have seen him, too, because the man gave his grizzly roar and took off out of the schoolhouse shouting, "I'm going to catch that boy."

Jake started to chuckle. The day was getting better all ready. Most people didn't think Higgins could move as fast as he could because he was so large, but the man used to say he'd learned to run by racing grizzly bears and Jake thought it just might be true.

Twenty minutes later Higgins was back holding a white-faced Elias Barker by the collar of his jacket.

"Now," Higgins said as he hauled Elias into the schoolroom. "You need to apologize to all of these good folks for scaring them."

"It wasn't only me," Elias protested.

"The others will apologize when I catch them," Higgins assured him. "This is your turn."

Elias muttered, "I'm sorry."

"There now," Higgins said as he gave the boy a little shake. "You sit down where you belong and pay attention to your schooling."

The boy's face went white. "I can't. My ma will tan my hide good. I'm not supposed to go to school with—" Elias stopped and swallowed.

The boy didn't finish his sentence, but he didn't need to for Jake to know what he'd been going to say. His mother didn't want him to go to school with Spotted Fawn.

"You leave your mother to me," Jake said as he started for the door.

"Wait."

He turned to see Elizabeth walking toward him.

"I'm coming with you," she said as she came even with him.

Jake liked having Elizabeth at his side as they went to talk to Mrs. Barker. She might be in mourning for another man, but she was standing by him in the ways she could. That had to count for something.

Chapter Thirteen

Mrs. Barker lived in a two-story frame house off the main street in town. Jake wondered if Elizabeth was comparing the woman's house to the one where they lived. He hoped not. Several loads of lumber had been used in the building of this house; the schoolhouse alone would have taken less than a third of the wood. And there were beveled glass windows in the front of the house that were for decoration alone. It made his house look damp and dark in comparison.

That being said, he didn't envy the Barkers. Not when he had Elizabeth by his side.

"Oh," Mrs. Barker said when she opened the door and saw who was there.

A man didn't need to know anything about elegance to know that the glimpse he had into the foyer of Mrs. Barker's house was about as fine as any sight he'd see around here. Even the banister on the stairs gleamed with polish.

"May we come inside?" Elizabeth asked.

Jake glanced down at his wife and noticed she wasn't looking to the inside of Mrs. Barker's house the way he was. No, Elizabeth was very proper. If he didn't know better, he would think she was on a social call. She had a polite smile on her face and a voice that sounded very formal.

"It's not really convenient right now," Mrs. Barker said as she crossed her arms.

Jake didn't much like the look of triumph on the older woman's face.

"It's about Elias," Elizabeth continued smoothly, however, as though she hadn't just been asked to leave.

"If it's about him going to that school, he won't be there until it's a fitting place for children to be." Mrs. Barker started to close the door.

That was enough, Jake told himself as he put his foot in the door. The time for politeness was over. "Is it fitting that the boy is running around almost getting himself shot?"

Well, that got Mrs. Barker's attention. She swung the door wide again. "What do you mean?"

"This nonsense has gone on for too long when a boy like Elias is setting off firecrackers to try and scare people. You know as well as I do, there are enough nervous men with guns in this town that the boy could get himself shot pulling stunts like that."

Mrs. Barker's face went a little pale. "He's all right, though, isn't he?"

Jake nodded. "Higgins ran him down and brought him back to the schoolhouse. Which is where he belongs."

"The children do need to be in school," Elizabeth added softly.

Mrs. Barker looked at them for a minute.

"I saw what you did with the schoolroom," she finally said with a sour twist to her mouth. "All those Christmas decorations."

"You're welcome to add some more to what's there," Elizabeth said. "The reverend has what's left of the paint we used. And there's lots of wall left."

"I did think you could use some more holly," Mrs. Barker said.

"Christmas is the time for goodwill," Elizabeth said. "Children especially always like Christmas. I know you don't want to ruin it for them. Can't we wait until after the holiday to sort everything else out?"

Mrs. Barker sighed. "I just want to make this a better town. I know it might not mean much to people like you, but having the railroad come here would make a big difference to most people in this town."

"The railroad won't mean anything if we don't find a way to get along better," Jake said. "Towns have split over things like this."

Mrs. Barker was quiet for another minute then she looked over at Elizabeth. "I suppose you're right. We can settle everything after Christmas. I'm sure no railroad representative will be out traveling this close to the holiday, anyway."

"Would you mind coming over and telling your son

that?" Jake asked. "He can let his friends know and, my guess is, they'll all be back in school this afternoon."

Mrs. Barker nodded. "I'll be over as soon as I get my hat."

"We'll see you there," Jake said as he took Elizabeth's arm. He didn't figure there was any need for her to be looking inside Mrs. Barker's house any longer than necessary. If he wasn't mistaken there was a window in the foyer that did nothing but look into another room. Who had so much money they could buy a glass window when they didn't even need to keep out any rain?

But Elizabeth must not have seen the window.

"She listened to us," Elizabeth said in amazement as she let Jake lead her down the steps of the Barker house. "I didn't think she'd listen to anyone."

"She cares about her son," Jake said.

"Well, of course, I can see that," Elizabeth said as they kept walking back to the schoolhouse.

"She's not giving up, you know," Jake added. "She just doesn't want to fight the children over Christmas."

Elizabeth knew how the woman felt. Every child deserved a happy Christmas.

The schoolhouse was noisy and crowded by the end of the day. Since so few of the children had been there in the morning, the reverend suggested Elizabeth and Virginia repeat what they'd said earlier about the pageant. By that time Elias was already rather loudly declaring that it was a dumb idea and Higgins was giving him his grizzly roar as a reminder to be polite—or, at least, silent.

"I still don't want to be no angel," Elias muttered, looking up at Higgins. "And nobody can make me be one, either."

Higgins snorted. "I can see that, boy. Only a fool would think you could behave well enough to pass for an angel. I'm just trying to get you to quiet down so people don't take you for something else entirely."

Elizabeth stepped closer to the man and the boy. She hadn't fully explained the pageant, but she didn't want any of the other children hearing the quarrel right now to follow Elias's lead. "If you don't want to be an angel, you can be something else then."

"Like what?"

Elizabeth looked to Virginia for help. "Ah, you could be a shepherd—"

"Nah, I don't want to be a shepherd, either. Sheep are dumb. Besides, I have a horse. Shepherds don't have horses."

"Well, then," Virginia said as she looked around the schoolroom. "Maybe you could be a star."

"Like in the sky?" Elias asked, obviously thinking about the idea.

"Even bigger and brighter than the ones you see in the sky now," Elizabeth said. "The Christmas star was a special star. Kings—remember 'We three kings from Orient are'? Well, these kings followed the star because it brought them to the Christ Child."

"So the star gets to tell the important people how to find things?" Elias asked. "Like a map for hidden treasure."

"In a way." Elizabeth paused. "I guess you could say

Jesus was a hidden treasure at first because no one knew where he was."

"Good," Elias said. "Could I ride my horse when I'm a star? He's a bay so he's kind of yellow."

"The pageant is inside. You know you can't ride your horse."

Several children rode horses to school each day and there were several posts at the side of the school where they could tie them.

Elias grinned. "It doesn't hurt to try. That's what my dad always says. If a man's got a good horse, he can do anything."

Elizabeth grinned back. "Even your dad knows a horse can't come inside the schoolhouse."

"I suppose."

Elizabeth decided Elias wasn't as much of a problem as she had thought. She looked at all the children. "We're going to have a wonderful Christmas. We'll enact the story of the birth of Jesus, we'll sing songs, we'll have—" She looked over at Virginia for help.

"We're hoping to have a tree, too," Virginia announced with delight. "You children would love to have a tree to decorate, wouldn't you? The school has to look like Christmas for our pageant."

The children were nodding and Elizabeth agreed. She'd love to have the inside of this room shining with Christmas cheer.

Mrs. Barker hadn't arrived yet to paint more decorations on the Miles City side of the wall, but Elizabeth intended to offer to help her when she showed up.

And if they were going to decorate more, they should have a tree.

None of the children had any reservations about having a Christmas tree. Almost all of them had heard about making ornaments even if they hadn't made any themselves.

"We'll ask the men to help us find a tree," Elizabeth said. "I'm sure whatever they find will do nicely. After all, the important thing is the joy we take in Christmas."

With that triumphant remark, Elizabeth and Virginia decided to let the children get back to their lessons. The two women walked out of the schoolhouse and stood on the steps.

"Well, at least they seem to like Christmas," Virginia said wearily. "I never knew a classroom of children could be so hard to manage."

"They'll do better when we start practicing," Elizabeth said as she put her hands on her back and stretched. She was a little sore from all of that scrubbing and painting yesterday. Her muscles weren't used to working after she'd lain in her tent for almost two weeks, doing nothing.

"We'll start in on the trees tomorrow," Virginia said. "I better get to Colter's place and start playing the piano."

Elizabeth nodded. She had things to do at home, as well.

Jake took Elizabeth and the baby home in the wagon and then rode off to go see Wells.

Two hours later, Elizabeth sat down in the rocking chair by the fire. Her hair was falling down and her clothes were all wet. She'd just finished washing that black mourning dress and she'd rather scrub the old canvas on her tent before she took her washboard to the dress again. The wet wool was heavy and it smelled bad.

Added to that she had made the mistake of using water that was hotter than she thought it was. The black dye turned her rinse water gray almost immediately. She'd had to wring the water out of the dress before she draped it over a chair that she'd placed close enough to the wood-stove so the dress would hopefully dry before tomorrow.

As odd as it was, Elizabeth admitted, she had an immense feeling of relief as she worked on that dress. She wanted to wear mourning. She wasn't ready to move on with her life and the dress helped her show that to everyone. It marked where she was. Somehow the dress slowed everything down so her feelings were once again equal with her life.

She would know who she was when she started wearing that dress. A wound needed a scab before it could heal properly and that dress was her scab.

Elizabeth sat and rocked for a few more minutes before she stood up and walked back to the stove. While the dress had been soaking earlier, she had started to bring in her canned goods from the lean-to and stack them against the far wall in the cabin. All of those jars of canned vegetables and preserves reminded her of who she was, as well. She was a strong woman who could provide for herself. She'd survive her mourning.

While she was bringing in the jars, she also brought in the red yarn and slipped it into her satchel that she kept at the foot of the bed. She had decided to use the red yarn to knit Christmas scarves for the baby and Spotted Fawn. The older girl took such delight in her hair ribbons she would surely like a bright red scarf to wear around her neck. And babies always liked bright colors.

She hadn't thought about what to get Jake for a present, but she planned to ask Annabelle's advice. She was almost certain the other woman was getting Higgins a Christmas present so she'd probably given the matter some thought.

Elizabeth almost envied Annabelle. The other woman seemed to accept things better than she did.

Elizabeth was not naive. She knew women often had to marry quickly to survive out here in the West. A man and a gun were almost necessary. But she did not want to be one of those women who married from necessity. She and Jake had an agreement that would be in place until spring, but she already knew he would let her stay and become a real wife to him if that's what she decided to do.

But she didn't want it to be that way. She wanted to be chosen. Oh, Jake had chosen her after a fashion. But he had been thinking of his nieces and not of himself. He would have married her no matter who she was. And he was much too kind to do anything but throw himself into their bargain.

She could spend the rest of her life with him and not know if he really wanted to be with her. Or she with him. She didn't want to risk that. She had learned with Matthew that it was very hard to live with a man she could not please. If she really got married again, she wanted the man to want to be with her. She didn't want to be some compromise he had made in life.

Besides, it would be good for her soul to grieve. She had lain in her tent, frozen in her anger at God, and now that she was out of her tent, she felt adrift. It's not that she'd forgiven God. She'd just kept going because there was nothing else to do.

She wasn't praying, not the way Jake did. He prayed as though God were his friend. When she started to pray lately the words stuck in her throat. She'd worn out her anger and it no longer felt as white-hot as it had. It had not gone away, though. It had just changed form into something cold and heavy and uncomfortable. In fact, it was very similar to that old mourning dress.

Just thinking of the dress reminded Elizabeth she should go turn the chair by the stove a little. She'd have to keep moving that chair all night if she expected the whole dress to be dry by tomorrow.

Well, supper would be coming before tomorrow, Elizabeth told herself as she stood up. She'd set some beans to soaking last night and they were ready to be cooked. She'd like to put a small jar of her tomatoes in with the beans. If she also chopped up another one of the onions Annabelle had given her, she'd have a good soup.

She'd noticed Jake liked his food spiced up with onions and maybe some black pepper flakes. She'd make him some corn bread, too. She had to admit she liked cooking for the man. Maybe it was because he never seemed to just assume there would be food on his plate as Matthew had done.

She shook her head. Is that what her days would be like, always comparing one man to the other? Surely, her heart should give her peace eventually.

Chapter Fourteen

The next day, Jake drove Elizabeth and the girls into town before it was full light. The frost was growing heavier each morning and he figured it would be good to get a stack of wood for the schoolhouse before the snows started. The reverend wasn't looking well enough to be out in the winter cutting firewood himself, anyway.

Besides, Jake felt like chopping wood today. He was trying to avoid looking at that mourning dress of Elizabeth's, but it was hard not to see it. He wondered if he was supposed to stop speaking to her while she was in this mourning of hers. It was a peculiar feeling to have his wife acting like a widow.

He knew right then that he had a problem. He needed to stop thinking of Elizabeth as his wife. They'd said their vows, but they'd only made a commitment until spring. He shook his head. He didn't know what to do with the mess he'd made of things. He never should have offered to let her go, but then she might never have agreed to stay.

He looked over at her and Elizabeth pulled her shawl more closely around her. She was moving away from him already.

Elizabeth could sense Jake was looking at her, but she didn't look up to meet his eyes. He hadn't said anything about the mourning dress even though she'd put it on for the first time to wear today. She'd taken a hot iron to it first, but it still looked a little rumpled. And it was itchy.

She knew it was unattractive. It was probably a good thing Matthew wasn't alive to see the dress; he would have made her tear it up for rags. Men could be so particular about things.

She quickly glanced sideways at Jake. "It's just for a season—the dress."

Jake grunted.

She was glad he didn't ask her how long the season would last. She wasn't sure what she would say. She had some things she wanted to finish with Matthew and she wasn't even sure what they were.

At least the brown shawl she wore covered most of her dress. She had unpacked the shawl yesterday; it was a thick winter one she'd used when she did her heavy work back in Kansas. She hadn't needed it on the journey and, when the fevers started, it had been easier to use a blanket. When she had lifted it out of its box she could almost still smell the dye she'd put into it early last fall. She'd boiled black walnut husks with a few late-season marigolds and the shawl had turned out a rich golden brown. She was grateful to have it now.

The schoolhouse was chilly when they all arrived. Spotted Fawn had been sitting in the back of the wagon with the baby so she was the last one to climb down from the wagon and go inside the schoolroom. No one else was there yet. Jake had said he wanted them to get there early so they could start fires in the two stoves so the reverend wouldn't need to do it before classes started.

Elizabeth held the baby inside her shawl while she bent over the book Spotted Fawn was showing her. The girl was already learning to read a few words and was carefully pronouncing them.

"That's wonderful," Elizabeth said and then beamed up at Jake as he closed the door on the second wood-stove. "Spotted Fawn can read!"

Jake walked over and put his arm on his niece's shoulder. He looked as if he was going to say something, but just then there were the sounds of footsteps on the porch.

"Someone's already here," a boy's voice protested from outside as something dropped on the wood.

Elizabeth looked at Jake. "That has to be Elias."

Jake nodded grimly. "I'll go see what he's up to."

Before Jake got to the door, however, it opened.

"Why, whatever—" Mrs. Barker said as she stood there in surprise. She had a handkerchief wrapped around her copper hair and a bucket of paint in one hand. She looked at Jake and Elizabeth. "What are you doing here at this hour of the morning?"

"Starting the fire," Jake said.

"I didn't think anyone would be here," Mrs. Barker

said. She had a blanket draped around herself and a well-worn work dress showing under that. "I don't normally go around looking like this."

"Don't worry about it," Elizabeth said. She was glad to see the other woman wasn't always so proper. "No one dresses up when they go to paint. I'm so glad you decided to help with the wall."

"Well," Mrs. Barker said with a twist to her lips. "It is Christmas. And Elias is quite taken with all of the stars. He wanted to add a couple of constellations to the wall. It won't be much paint so we thought it would be okay if we did it before school today."

By this time Elias was inside the schoolroom, as well. He carried a couple of small paintbrushes. For once, he wasn't scowling.

"I thought maybe the Big Dipper," Elias said. "I like that one."

"I like it, too," Jake said as he walked over to the boy. "If you want any help getting the distances right, let me know."

Well, Elizabeth thought, a person just never knew what would happen in a day.

Elizabeth helped Mrs. Barker get the paint opened and stirred while Jake and Elias marked the places on the wall where they wanted their stars.

"It was good of you to do this," Mrs. Barker finally said. "All of the stars and other Christmas decorations are nice."

Elizabeth nodded. She refused to ask the other woman if she was the one who had painted that awful black line. It had to have been her. Who else would have done it? But if Elizabeth asked the question she was pretty sure it would destroy any fragile truce they had managed.

"We'll wait until after Christmas for—" Mrs. Barker said with a nod of her head at Spotted Fawn.

"She is not harming anyone," Elizabeth said, trying to keep her voice low and mild. She didn't want to let the remark pass, but she didn't want to distress Spotted Fawn, either, so she didn't want the girl to hear their voices.

"We've got the places marked," Elias called out excitedly.

Mrs. Barker took the paint over to Elias and Jake.

"He's having fun," Elizabeth said when the other woman returned to where they had been standing.

Mrs. Barker nodded. "It's good for him to spend some time with a man. Boys like that and his father has been away for such a long time."

"Oh, I'm sorry. I didn't know."

"He's off prospecting again. He made one big strike. You'd think that would be enough for the man. We have everything we need, but he's off again. Someplace over by Helena, the last time he wrote."

"Well, I'm sure he'll be home soon," Elizabeth said. She didn't want to feel sympathy for the other woman, but she did.

"I keep thinking that, if the railroad comes, there would be a good job that would keep him here. A boy needs his father."

And a wife needs her husband, Elizabeth thought, until the irony of it struck her.

By the time the reverend got to the school, several constellations were painted and the chill had been taken off the morning air.

"Oh, the children will be so pleased," the reverend said as he admired the additional stars. "That's excellent work, Elias."

The boy ducked his head. His face was pink with pleased embarrassment.

"I think everyone would agree that Miles City is keeping up their end of things," Mrs. Barker said proudly.

"It's not a competition," Elizabeth protested. "It's Christmas."

"Still, people have certain expectations of the people of Miles City that they naturally don't have of the people of Dry Creek."

"I don't think—" Elizabeth began.

"Ladies," Reverend Olson interrupted hastily. "You have both given us wonderful decorations. And the children are so excited about the Christmas tree you mentioned."

"There's going to be a Christmas tree?" Mrs. Barker frowned. "Elias didn't tell me there was going to be a tree."

"It won't be a big tree," Elizabeth said. "Jake says he thinks there are a few short pines not too far east of here, down some ravine. He's going to bring a small one back for us."

Elizabeth had been delighted when Jake had heard them talking and offered to bring them the tree. She had never known a man before who bothered with the dreams of children.

"Well, if we have a tree, we want to have a proper one. My husband used to say there were some fine-looking pines north of here someplace. He and Elias saw them when they were out riding one day. I'm sure Elias remembers. It's quite a ways from here I think, but maybe he could tell one of the men where it is and—"

"I'm sure Jake will talk to him," Elizabeth said. "But it's likely too far. I'm sure if there's anything close, Jake would know about it. Besides, a simple tree is fine. Just something so the children can make ornaments."

"Oh, dear, no," Mrs. Barker said. "I don't think we want a small little tree to represent our town. We have a certain reputation, after all."

Elizabeth figured the other woman would stop worrying as the day went on, but she was wrong. By the time Elizabeth and Virginia were ready to help the students make ornaments, Mrs. Barker was back at the schoolhouse, this time dressed in a mauve silk dress and matching hat.

Annabelle had offered to keep the baby at the store with her while Elizabeth and Virginia worked on Christmas with the children so Elizabeth was able to give her complete focus to the ornaments. Unfortunately, focus hadn't been enough.

"I guess people generally use red paper," Elizabeth said as she and Virginia looked at the rope of white paper that the students had made. The decoration was sitting on top of the teacher's desk. The loops in the rope were uneven and, instead of looking charming, it gave the whole thing the appearance of being fought over by a couple of dogs.

"I don't suppose we could paint the paper with something," Virginia asked.

"Oh, of course not," Mrs. Barker said as she walked over to where they stood. "Any kind of paint we have would wrinkle the paper even more. You need to let me buy us some decorations. The children have better things to do than decorate a Christmas tree, anyway."

"We can't buy Christmas," Elizabeth protested. "The children have as much right to decorate a tree as anyone here."

"Ladies," the reverend interrupted gently.

Elizabeth looked behind her to see the children all looking at her and Mrs. Barker. Some of the younger girls had big eyes and even the boys were looking a little stunned.

"Of course, the important thing about Christmas is that we all get along," Elizabeth said as she forced a big smile onto her face.

Then Elizabeth walked right over to Mrs. Barker and gave her a hug.

The other woman gasped, but Elizabeth knew there was nothing Mrs. Barker could do but adjust her hat and smile back.

"And, don't worry," Elizabeth said to the children as she turned to face. "Miss Virginia and I are going over to the store right now to see what we can get to use to make better ornaments. We'll be back."

With that Elizabeth swept out of the room, with Virginia following her.

"Do you think Annabelle will let us owe the money for a week or so?" Virginia asked as they started walking down the street. "I don't make enough to do more than pay for my room and board. Although Colter has said all along that I could use the piano to start giving lessons to people. Maybe then I'd have extra—"

Elizabeth stopped. "The piano in the saloon?"

It was the middle of the afternoon and the streets of Miles City were dry, but quiet.

Virginia nodded. "So, of course, it would have to be an adult for them to have the lessons."

Elizabeth shook her head. "We need to find you a different job. I'm sure you could find children who would want to take piano lessons, but their parents will never send them to that place to take them."

"I know," Virginia sighed. "But, even if I had a room someplace, I would need a piano. I've been praying, but—"

"I know." Elizabeth pursed her lips. Finally, someone else understood. "God just doesn't answer."

Virginia looked startled. "That's not what I was going to say. I was just going to say He hasn't told me my next step yet."

"Oh," Elizabeth said.

"I can understand how you feel," Virginia said softly. "I'm still grieving for my brother, too."

Elizabeth nodded. "I can't get past it. The whole thing is just a knot inside of me. That's why I'm wearing this mourning dress. I need to find a way past everything if I'm going to stay with Jake."

"Well, I'll pray you do that then," Virginia said as they reached the boardwalk in front of the mercantile. "It's not everyone that gets a second chance at happiness."

When they walked inside the store, Annabelle walked out from behind her counter and greeted them. "The baby's asleep in the back if that's why you've come."

Elizabeth shook her head. She'd already been over to nurse.

"We want something to make into Christmas ornaments," Virginia said.

Annabelle motioned for them to follow her over to a shelf. "We do have some of the most beautiful hand-blown ornaments, if you decide not to make them yourselves."

Annabelle pulled a box off the shelf and opened it.

"Ohhh," Elizabeth said. Beautiful glass apples shone there. And shiny pinecones. And clusters of red berries.

"They're expensive, of course. The owners ordered them from the Greiner's factory in Germany. They were supposed to be on our shelves last Christmas, but they got stuck in the docks in New York and missed some railroad connection so we saved them to sell this Christmas."

The ornaments were molded into the shapes of fruits and nuts.

"They're lovely," Virginia sighed.

"But we're thinking more of something to use so the students here can make their own ornaments." Elizabeth added.

"Well, if that's what you want, the best thing is right here."

With that, Annabelle went behind the counter, reached down inside the clerk's space and pulled out the Turkey red calico cloth that Elizabeth had dyed.

"I know this cloth has special meaning to you," Annabelle said. "But ornaments wouldn't use much of it. And it would make lovely ornaments—it's got that strong Christmas red color."

"Oh, that's the perfect thing to do with it," Elizabeth said.

"I still don't know how you managed to get it so the color would stay," Annabelle said.

"It was simple enough." Elizabeth grinned. "I boiled the cloth in alkali and let it sit in a tub of soured oil before I dunked it in the dye."

Virginia wrinkled her nose.

Elizabeth nodded. "I had to do it outdoors. Matthew refused to walk near the tub. It did smell pretty bad."

She might wear this mourning dress in memory of Matthew, but her heart would ease some on her daughter's death if the children made Christmas ornaments out of Rose's cloth. She knew the bright red cloth ornaments would have delighted Rose if she could see them.

"Still, Matthew must have been proud of you. Knowing how to do something like that," Annabelle said.

Elizabeth shook her head. "It embarrassed him that I was doing what he called servant work."

"I didn't know you had servants."

Elizabeth laughed. "Oh, we didn't have the money

for something like that. Matthew just wanted us to live like we had servants. Which meant I had to do so many things when he wasn't looking. Unfortunately dyeing wasn't something that could be done when he was away for an hour or so."

"Well, he should have been proud of you for doing what you did," Annabelle protested staunchly. "Not every woman knows how to dye her own cloth."

"It wasn't just that the smells were bad," Elizabeth said. "He didn't like that my hands sometimes wore a stain for days afterward. I tried to be careful, but it is hard to dye things without getting any of the dye on you."

"Well, Jake would have been proud," Annabelle said. "It's quite something what you can do."

Elizabeth smiled. "I used to be so taken away when I was dyeing things. To be able to turn something plain into something beautiful is—well, it's hard to describe. One good dunking and everything looks different."

"It's like getting a second chance," Virginia said. "Like with redemption. You know, in the Bible."

"I suppose it is at that."

When they got back to the schoolroom, Mrs. Barker had gone. Elizabeth showed the children the cloth and Virginia started to cut some of it into strips so the children could make bright red Christmas braids for the tree.

When Virginia told everyone that Elizabeth had dyed the cloth herself, the children were impressed.

"Maybe we can dye some of the costumes for the pageant," Elizabeth said, looking to Reverend Olson for approval. "We'd have to do it outside, of course, and only the adults could actually do the dyeing. But it is interesting."

The reverend nodded. "I'm sure my wife would like to see this, too. Not too many people dye things anymore. It's quite the art."

Elizabeth beamed. No one had ever called her dyed fabrics art before.

She'd thought about what Virginia had said earlier, about her dyeing cloth being like a redemptive second chance. She wondered if God ever felt the way she did after she'd taken something gray and sorrowful and given it a new life. She hoped He did. Maybe He could do that with the angry hurt inside of her.

Chapter Fifteen

Two days later, Jake was chopping wood again behind the schoolhouse. He had found a small pine tree the day before and dragged it up from the ravine. The tree wasn't higher than four feet tall. He knew Elias was convinced there was a ten-foot tree out there somewhere, but Jake knew there wasn't a pine tree that tall closer than the ponderosas in the Black Hills and even the soldiers weren't making that trip right now.

There were rumors that the renegades were banding together to make some final attacks before winter set in. Of course, everyone was probably safe this close to the fort. There were not that many renegades even if they all came together for an attack.

Jake told all of that to Elias, but the boy repeated his claim with a fervor made more adamant by his obvious wish that his father was here to back him up and his mother's misguided statements that even an eight-foot-tall tree would solve everyone's Christmas troubles. She considered the four-foot-tall tree they had in the school-house to be no better than a bush.

Jake had no patience with any of it. He knew no tree would solve his trouble. Unless, of course, he could chop it up into kindling and use it to burn that old mourning dress his wife was wearing.

"Here, let me carry that," he said as he saw Elizabeth walking around the side of the schoolhouse pulling an old scrubbing tub.

"Thanks," Elizabeth said as she stopped and tried to catch her breath.

"You should have called me earlier," Jake said as he picked up the tub and balanced it on his shoulder. "That's what you have a husband for."

"Oh." Elizabeth was still wearing that drab mourning dress, but she blushed like a young girl.

Jake didn't even try to hide his grin. "I'm guessing this tub has something to do with Christmas?"

Elizabeth nodded and her eyes lit up. "We're going to dye some of the costumes for the pageant. I thought it would be a good chance to show the children how clothes are dyed. Some of them have never seen it done."

"You know, I don't think I've ever seen it, either," Jake said. He needed a break from chopping wood about now anyway. "Maybe I could use a little education, too."

"You're interested in dyeing?" Elizabeth asked, the delight evident in her face. "Most men don't pay any attention to that kind of thing."

"Out here, men need to know a lot of different things."

Elizabeth nodded. "You can help me build the fires

then. We'll need three of them. One for the yellow. One for the brown. And the tub of soda ash for getting the angel costumes a little more white. Well, and setting the other colors, too."

Jake nodded. It was a good thing he and Colter were chopping firewood the way they were. They were going to need it.

Elizabeth walked back into the schoolhouse and stood for a minute in the doorway. The children had spent so many hours making ornaments lately and practicing their songs for the pageant that they had spread out to cover both halves of the room. She had noticed the young Larson girl was even chatting away with Spotted Fawn yesterday during recess. Elizabeth figured it was difficult to continue being afraid of Spotted Fawn when the children saw how much effort she was putting into pronouncing the names right in her McGuffy Reader.

Jake had watched Elizabeth walk around the schoolhouse before he turned and looked for several good places to put her dyeing tubs. The schoolhouse was on the edge of town and, standing behind it, a man could see for miles. A few cottonwoods were scattered here and there and there was a fair-sized ravine that ran fairly close to the school. He suspected the boys had some good games with each other, hiding in that ravine.

Jake decided to set the tubs up a few yards from the school. He had barely cleared the second spot of dead grass when Colter walked around the schoolhouse carrying his ax. Jake glanced up and knew something was wrong. He'd seen the other man frown a fair amount, but he'd never seen him looking so thunderous.

"Problems?" Jake asked.

Colter grunted as he walked past Jake and went to a log that was lying near the woodpile.

Jake followed the other man over. "You didn't overhear any other pranks the boys are planning, did you?"

Colter shook his head as he positioned himself in front of the log to take a swing with his ax. "Nope. But I found out who's been robbing the till."

Jake watched as the other man took a powerful swing at the log with the ax, chopping it cleanly into two pieces.

"The bartender?"

Colter shook his head as he moved to take another swing. "Danny."

Jake stood there in sympathy as the ax hit the wood. "You're sure?"

Colter turned and looked at Jake fully for the first time. "I caught him at it. He didn't deny it, either. He told me he was taking the money so he could buy Miss Virginia her own piano." Colter's lips twisted into a bitter smile. "That's why he stole that watch, too. It seems Danny doesn't think Miss Virginia should play the piano in my fine establishment. He thinks she should have her own place where she can give piano lessons to people without them needing to come to a saloon."

"Ahh," Jake said.

Colter glared at Jake. "I suppose you agree with Danny."

Jake shrugged. "A woman like Virginia knows how

to behave no matter where she is, but I do think she'd get more students if she was in her own place."

As the two men stood there for a minute longer, the fight went out of Colter.

"Don't you think I know that?" Colter said. "But she doesn't have money to buy her own piano. How's she going to set herself up in business?"

"Maybe some of us could get together and loan her the money," Jake said.

"You know she'd never take it," Colter said. "Before she even started working at my place, I offered to give her some money. She was so indignant you'd have thought I was offering to buy her virtue."

"Were you?" Jake asked softly. He knew the way men like Colter operated.

Colter shook his head. "I didn't intend it at the time, but, well—I've never known a woman like Virginia before. She's—" Colter swallowed. "The truth is I don't know what she is, but I do know Danny is right. She doesn't belong in my place playing piano for a bunch of depressed men who've got nothing better to do than drink themselves into an early grave. She doesn't belong anywhere around men like that—or, ones like me."

With that, Colter sank his ax into the tree log and stomped off.

Give the poor man grace, Lord, Jake prayed as he watched Colter walk around the side of the school-house. He figured Colter knew he didn't stand much chance with Virginia, but the man still wanted to help

her to a better life. A man who didn't know how to help
the woman he loved was a miserable man indeed.

Jake decided he could use some of that grace himself.
He had spent more time these last few days resenting
that old mourning dress his wife was wearing than
asking himself how he could help her with her grief.
Whether she decided she wanted to be married to him
or not, he owed her the concern he would give to anyone
else who had seen someone they loved die.

It was afternoon before Elizabeth had everything
ready for the children to watch their costumes being
dyed. Before she had left the house that morning, she'd
put all of the old union suits in the back of the wagon so
she'd have them in school today. There were nineteen
union suits and seventeen children in the pageant. Some
of the union suits needed to be cut and some cinched with
a rope so they'd stay on, but each child had their own and
brought it out behind the schoolhouse to be dyed.

The sun was shining today and the children were
comfortable outside.

"Stand back," Elizabeth said as the children came too
close to the tub she had boiling. "This first dye is yellow
for the stars."

"Take mine first," Tommy said.

Elizabeth accepted Tommy's union suit and put it in
the boiling water. She had dried petals of goldenrod
and marigolds in there.

While Elizabeth was dyeing the yellow suits, Jake
put up another tub a few yards away. Soda ash was

stirred into the boiling water in that tub. The limestone-and-salt mixture would help set the yellow dye and whiten the angel costumes.

The last tub, filled with water and the husks from black walnut shells, was boiling away. That dye would make the shepherd's costumes a nice brown.

It would take most of the afternoon to finish the dyeing and Elizabeth was amazed that Jake helped her with the stirring. The yellow and soda ash tubs didn't smell too bad, but most people didn't like to go too close to any of it.

Jake was in love. He'd known it before, but watching Elizabeth and her dyes made him proud of his wife. She showed a reverence for the whole process that made the children feel as though they were part of an important moment. And Jake agreed that they were. His wife knew how to change things. She was taking those old union suits and making them into costumes that were exciting the children.

"I think we want a little more yellow for your star, Elias, don't you?" Elizabeth asked as she held up the boy's costume. "After all you are the brightest star in the sky."

Elias nodded.

Jake wondered how his wife had managed to take this schoolroom full of students who just last week were sitting on opposite sides of each other and make them into one excited group of kids pulling together to have just the right colors.

Jake stayed through all of the dyeing and watched as

finally each child had a wet union suit in a different color that they were holding close enough to them so they could see what each other looked like.

"Look, Spotted Fawn isn't brown no more—and Elias is yellow," the Larson girl said with a giggle.

Jake almost said something, but he saw Elizabeth turn to the girl.

"That's the way it is with most color," Elizabeth said as she looked over all of the children with satisfaction in her eyes. "Color is usually just on the outside. Inside most things are the same."

"Hair's that way, too," Tommy said. "Elias got his in red and I got mine in brown."

"I've always said God likes color," Elizabeth agreed as she motioned for the children to bring their union suits to the rope she'd tied between two of the closer cottonwood trees. "We'll just let these dry while we go back inside and practice your songs for the pageant."

Jake watched the children walk around the side of the schoolhouse. He couldn't help but notice they walked a little closer to Spotted Fawn than they usually did.

Jake realized he'd married a miracle worker. He didn't know if his wife had set out to teach the children a lesson on the color of everyone's skin, but he had a hunch she had known exactly what she was doing. It made him feel humble. And even more sympathetic than before to Colter.

Elizabeth had left some bean soup simmering on the back of the cookstove when she'd left in the morning so, by the time she, Jake, Spotted Fawn and the baby came back to the cabin late that afternoon, supper was almost ready.

"Just let me see to the horses," Jake said as he helped Elizabeth down from the wagon.

Jake guided the horses closer to the lean-to once Elizabeth and Spotted Fawn were inside his cabin. He wanted to unload a few things without anyone seeing. When the wagon was still, he stepped down and folded back the furs that had been lying behind the seat.

He had a mirror and hairbrush for Spotted Fawn for Christmas and a small music box for the baby. Annabelle had wrapped them both in bright pieces of cloth when he bought them in the mercantile this afternoon. He'd searched the shelves for something fitting for Elizabeth, but he hadn't found anything. He had gone to the telegraph office, however, and put in an order for a large piece of pink granite for that headstone he had promised her.

The girls' presents were to be a surprise, but the headstone wasn't. He planned to tell Elizabeth that he'd ordered it; he just didn't want to talk about it in front of the children. He knew that Spotted Fawn had grown close to Elizabeth. He didn't want his niece to worry that, once the gravestone was completed, Elizabeth would leave them.

Although, he had to admit, his niece might be right to think that. Jake spent a few extra minutes taking the presents up to his loft area before walking back to the cabin door.

Elizabeth added a little more salt to the bean soup. She would let the soup finish cooking while she put the leftover biscuits from breakfast into the oven to heat.

"My angel costume is the whitest," Spotted Fawn said as she walked over to the stove. "Even Elias says so."

Elizabeth smiled as she slid the cold biscuits onto a tin plate. "Christmas is not a competition. It's our Lord's birthday. But I am glad to see you are making some friends."

Spotted Fawn shook her head emphatically. "Elias is not my friend, he's my enemy."

Elizabeth opened the door next to the stove's firebox and put the biscuits inside. "Well, sometimes enemies can become friends. It takes more effort, of course, but the Bible talks about it."

Jake walked through the door.

"What does the Bible talk about?" he asked as he took off his coat.

"Making friends out of enemies." Spotted Fawn frowned. "I'm not sure it can be done." She looked up at Jake.

Jake nodded. "You'll even be able to read about it yourself. I'll show you where it talks about it tonight when I come up to say good-night."

"Supper will be ready soon," Elizabeth said as she turned away from the stove.

An hour later, Jake sighed in contentment. They were all seated at the table, although Elizabeth looked as if she was ready to get up again.

Jake stood and put his hand on his wife's shoulder.

"You sit a bit more. I'll start the water heating for dishes. You've had a busy day."

Elizabeth nodded. "But you still don't have to—I mean, I'm perfectly able to wash a few dishes."

"So am I," Jake said as he bent down and picked up the dish tub from the bottom shelf. "Maybe they won't come out a different color than they were when I started, like you did today with those costumes. But I can get something clean enough."

"Even the browns turned out pretty good," Elizabeth said as she stood up. "And it's hard to get a true color in browns."

Eventually, Jake and Elizabeth decided to do the dishes together. Elizabeth was washing and Jake was drying the dishes with a piece of flannel. When he'd done dishes in the old days, he'd give them a good dunking in hot water and set them back on the shelves. But drying dishes was nice. He got to stand close enough to Elizabeth that their hips were always touching.

Spotted Fawn was rocking the baby to sleep so Jake kept his voice low so only Elizabeth could hear.

"I lost my mother, you know," Jake said quietly. "I know how it is to lose someone you love."

Elizabeth looked up from the dishwater in surprise.

"If there's anything I can do to help you grieve, let me know," Jake continued. He might not be overly fond of that black dress, but he was surely attached to the woman who was wearing it.

Elizabeth blinked. "Thank you, I—well, thank you."

"I ordered the headstone today. Granite, like I promised."

"Oh."

"It won't be here until after Christmas, but I'll start to carving as soon as it comes." Jake figured that finishing that headstone was the one clear thing he could do to help his wife in her grief.

"I'm obliged," Elizabeth said.

Jake nodded as he went back to drying dishes. He hadn't known what simple pleasures were to be had when there was a woman like Elizabeth in his house.

"You did a fine thing this afternoon," Jake said as he folded his flannel cloth and set it on the shelf. "Dyeing the costumes for the children and helping them to see that God has made us all different and yet the same."

"Well, it's true," Elizabeth said and then hesitated. "Your baby niece taught me that."

"I wish the parents of those children could learn the lesson, too."

Elizabeth winced. "I think Mrs. Barker is getting worse, not better. She was at the school this afternoon and I could tell she was trying to get the children to sit on the Miles City side of the room. The reverend kept them up doing sums at the board and then Virginia had them singing, so we just didn't let anyone sit down much. But we can't keep that up."

Jake nodded. It was hard to worry about Mrs. Barker when he noticed how delicate his wife's neck was with that loose strand of hair falling down like it was. That mourning dress might be all that was ugly, but it showed off Elizabeth's skin for the beauty it was.

Chapter Sixteen

It was Thursday of the next week before the alterations were made on the costumes and the children could all hit the high notes in the Christmas carols they were practicing for the pageant. Sunday had come and gone with no thaw in the line that separated Miles City from Dry Creek in church. Elizabeth was unhappy about that. She didn't like to see conflict in the church and, added to that, there were only a few people who came to sit on the Miles City side. Mrs. Barker and her friends stayed away.

The Reverend Olson just carried on as if the whole church was in attendance.

Elizabeth asked him about that on Wednesday.

"God would rather people speak their minds than just go home and complain about the church's policy on something," he said.

Elizabeth was helping the reverend get ready for school to start. Spotted Fawn and the baby were in the back of the room and Jake was outside getting some wood for the fires.

"I always thought it was disrespectful to show that kind of anger to God," she said, a little hesitantly.

The reverend chuckled. "I'm sure God has seen more anger in His time than any one of us can possibly imagine."

Elizabeth took a breath. This was her chance. "When my baby died, I was afraid to tell God I was angry for fear He'd punish me and not let me see her again, not even in Heaven."

"Oh, dear," the reverend said. "God isn't interested in punishing you for your feelings. He knows you are grieving for your baby."

Elizabeth blinked.

"If you want to cry, that's fine," the reverend said.

Elizabeth shook her head. "I don't cry."

Just then Jake stepped inside and the reverend called him over.

"It's time to comfort each other," the reverend said as Jake stepped closer. "That's what being married is about."

Elizabeth stiffened. But Jake just put his arms around her and drew her to him. He had been outside and his clothes were cold and a little damp. He was wearing his wool shirt, though and, once it warmed up, it was soft and nice.

Jake didn't seem to want anything but to hold her so Elizabeth relaxed against him.

"The reverend and I were just talking," Elizabeth mumbled against Jake's chest. "About Rose and Matthew."

"I know," he said as he pulled her closer. "I know."

"I don't think I can forget about them."

Jake pressed a kiss to the top of her head. "You don't have to. Just add me and the girls to them."

If there weren't more footsteps on the porch outside the schoolhouse, Elizabeth thought she would never have moved away from Jake's arms. As it was, she took the feel of his arms with her throughout the rest of the day.

Later that day, Elizabeth taught the angels to fly. Colter had given them some smooth wire he had in the back room at his place and Virginia bent the wire into the shape of wings for each of the angels while Elizabeth took the angels, once they had wings, and taught them how to walk without doing damage to anyone passing by. The children called it learning to fly.

"Well, I get to be a blazing star," Elias said as he went over to twist a bit on Spotted Fawn's wings. The girl turned to glare at him.

Elizabeth's heart sang at the sight. Elias was treating Spotted Fawn just the way he treated the other girls. Spotted Fawn might not see his actions as being friendly, but Elizabeth knew it was a big step forward for the boy.

"Now, children," Elizabeth said, her voice all that was proper.

Virginia finished fashioning the last of the angel wings and stepped over to where Elizabeth was.

"I think we're going to be ready," Virginia said.

Elizabeth nodded. It was Wednesday and the pageant was set for Friday evening. "I think it's going to be wonderful."

The angels were in tune, the shepherds had all found an old tree branch to use as a staff, and the stars had practiced looking wise for the procession. Annabelle and Higgins were going to play Mary and Joseph.

The short Christmas tree was decorated with stars and wreaths cut out of Rose's red calico. It might not be a glamorous tree, but it had been made with the love of little fingers. The reverend was calling the class back to attention so Elizabeth and Virginia quietly went outside on the steps of the school. The air was chilly, but not as cold as it had been. The sky was overcast, though, and the whole town of Miles City looked gray and muddy.

"Not very much like Christmas out here," Virginia said. "I keep telling Colter he needs to put some decorations up in his window, but he keeps saying that's not the kind of place he runs."

"I suppose it isn't."

Virginia nodded unhappily. "I wish it was."

"I know," Elizabeth put her hand on her friend's arm.

Just then they both heard a woman's shriek.

"What was that?" Elizabeth said as she started down the steps with Virginia following right behind her.

The two women were at the bottom of the steps and walking toward the street when they saw Mrs. Barker coming straight toward them, waving a small piece of paper in her hand.

"This is terrible," she shouted from the street as she marched her way toward them.

"What did we do now?" Virginia asked.

"Nothing," Elizabeth said. She hoped that was true. "We've done nothing she can object to."

Mrs. Barker's face was red and her breath was coming fast when she got to the schoolhouse steps. Her hat was a little crooked and her eyes were panicked.

"Oh, dear." Elizabeth took an instinctive step forward. "What's wrong?"

Mrs. Barker took a deep breath and then wailed, "He's coming."

Elizabeth looked at Virginia, but the other woman was of no help.

"Mr. Barker?" Elizabeth asked. She couldn't think of any other man who would get this reaction from Mrs. Barker.

The older woman shook her head. "No, the railroad man. I just got a telegraph from my cousin. The railroad man will be here Friday night. Somehow he heard about our Christmas pageant and he decided it would be a good time to visit."

"He heard about our Christmas pageant?" Virginia said, looking pleased. "Well, isn't that nice?"

Mrs. Barker glared at her. "It's a disaster is what it is."

With that Mrs. Barker started marching toward the schoolhouse door.

"Wait," Elizabeth called after her, trying to stop the woman. "School is in—"

It was too late; Mrs. Barker had opened the school-house door.

Jake was walking back from the mercantile, his

Christmas present for Elizabeth securely tucked away in his shirt pocket, when he heard the commotion over at the schoolhouse.

The schoolhouse door was open and Jake walked right inside.

"We're ruined, just ruined," Mrs. Barker said, wringing her hands at the front of the classroom. "Just look at this—we've got paint all over and we don't even have a proper Christmas tree. That railroad man is going to take one look at us and decide not to come near us."

"Surely he knows it's a children's pageant," the reverend said. "He can't expect it to be perfect."

"He'll at least expect a proper Christmas tree," Mrs. Barker wailed. "I had such high hopes for the railroad coming."

Elizabeth stepped over to put her arm around Mrs. Barker. "There. There. It will be fine."

"What do you know?" Mrs. Barker pulled back. "Your husband is here. You don't have to make this a better place so he'll come home."

"I'm sure the railroad man will understand," Elizabeth repeated quietly. "We'll just do what we can to make him comfortable. And I've already planned to make a big batch of my fried apple doughnuts. I've never known a man to turn one of those down. And I promised Wells I'd make some pecan pies. And maybe some fruit bread for everyone."

"See, it'll be a feast," the reverend said as he patted Mrs. Barker on the back. "He probably won't even notice the tree."

With that, Mrs. Barker let out a sob and ran from the schoolroom.

There was silence when she slammed the door behind her.

"Now I don't want any of you children to worry," the reverend finally said. "We're not doing this pageant to impress the railroad man. We're doing it to the glory of God and that's all we need to worry about."

Jake could see right then that the children weren't as worried about the glory of God as they were about pleasing Mrs. Barker. Well, he couldn't blame them. He'd never been inclined to do battle with the woman, either. She could sure take the joy out of Christmas.

That afternoon, Virginia stayed at school to help the children practice and Elizabeth went home to begin her baking. She stopped by the mercantile to pick up the baby, of course, but she also wanted to get a bottle of vanilla to use in her doughnuts.

"What's happening over there?" Annabelle asked when Elizabeth walked into the store. "Mrs. Barker was just here and she bought every one of those Christmas ornaments we had—the imported ones. All two dozen of them. They cost a small fortune."

"Well, I'm not surprised," Elizabeth said as she stood in front of the counter. "The railroad man is apparently coming to see the children's pageant and Mrs. Barker is convinced we'll look so bad the railroad will never come."

"I doubt the railroad is worried about whether or not the children can sing," Annabelle said.

Elizabeth smiled. "I think we'll do all right in the

singing. Virginia is singing along with the children and
she has the voice of an angel. No, it's the tree and probably
the children's costumes that are upsetting Mrs. Barker
most."

Annabelle grinned. "Well, I suppose angels don't
really wear union suits."

Elizabeth chuckled. "Neither do the stars. Shepherds
might, though."

"Well, it will all work out fine," Annabelle said. "Especially now that you have Higgins up on stage to make
sure the boys behave."

Elizabeth nodded. "I'm thinking the look of awe in
the shepherds' faces will have more to do with Higgins
than the devotion the boys have for the Christ child."

Annabelle laughed. "Clarence does enjoy going to
school with the boys."

"Clarence, is it now?"

Annabelle blushed. "He's asked me to marry him."

"Oh, I'm so happy for you. He's a good man."

Annabelle nodded. "I know."

Elizabeth took the happiness of her conversation with
Annabelle home with her. Her friend and Higgins hadn't
publicly announced their plans yet so Elizabeth didn't tell
Jake. He'd let Higgins tell his friend. Once Jake did know
she planned to ask him if they could shivaree the couple
just like Higgins and Wells had done with the two of them.

Elizabeth made enough fried apple doughnuts that
afternoon so that she could take some to the children.
The pageant was coming tomorrow and she wanted
them to relax and concentrate on pleasing their parents

with the performance. She realized this would be the first time the adults of Miles City and Dry Creek would sit together since they'd parted over that black line down the middle of the floor. None of the parents would refuse to come to the pageant because of where they might have to sit.

Surely, the parents were more important than some railroad man.

Before she went to bed that night, she baked some ginger cookies, too. She was determined to do whatever she could to make sure the pageant was a success. If that meant she had to stay up late baking, then so be it. She'd cooked for enough people in her life to know that people were more civilized with each other when they were well fed.

She'd have to take a basket of cookies to the school, as well as the doughnuts. Food worked on children just as it did on their parents.

She was slipping the last cookies from the oven when it occurred to her that maybe she had a tendency to rely on her cooking too much. She'd spent so much of her life taking care of herself that she never had found it natural to turn to God with her troubles. And then, after Matthew and Rose, it was even harder.

She'd been seeing God a little differently of late. Maybe if He believed in dyeing people the way she believed in renewing cloth, then maybe He was worried about people getting along as much as she was. Maybe He wasn't just up there with the stars. Maybe He was down here with her, as well.

But, of course, she thought to herself with a rueful smile, that was what Christmas was about, after all. Even Spotted Fawn had been asking more questions about how to make Elias her friend instead of her enemy.

Now, if only the adults in Miles City could ask the same questions, this Christmas would really be a time of love and goodwill.

Chapter Seventeen

Friday morning was overcast. The sky had been getting a darker gray for the past few days and Jake was predicting a snowstorm before Sunday, which was Christmas Day. As long as the snow waited until then to fall, she would welcome it, Elizabeth told herself as she sat by the fire, rocking the baby. The baby had finished nursing and Elizabeth snuggled her closer. The thought of being snowed in with her little family for the holiday sounded very pleasant.

But first, all of the families needed to go to the pageant and, for that, bare ground would be helpful. Elizabeth put the baby in the crib. She had heard enough about the snowstorms that came to this area to realize no one wanted to travel during them. Virginia said the snow could be five feet tall around the fort some winter days.

Elizabeth didn't want to think about any snowbanks that were as high as that. She did make Spotted Fawn take a blanket with her when she rode her pony to school, though. Elizabeth and Jake would be taking the wagon in later so they would bring Spotted Fawn home after school or Elizabeth wouldn't have even let the girl ride this morning.

But Jake had assured them both that the storm was at least hours away and his horses could pull a wagon home through the snow if it came later.

Still, Elizabeth worked quickly to finish baking the last batch of pies.

Spotted Fawn had her angel costume with her in a pouch she carried on her pony. She'd also asked Elizabeth for some yarn to tie things and so she had a ball of yellow yarn as well as some hair ribbons. Elizabeth suspected the girl was putting together some kind of presents. Elizabeth even tucked a small ball of the red yarn in with the yellow in case the girl wanted anything to look like Christmas.

Elizabeth hadn't thought of a gift for Jake yet, so she needed to take some time today to visit the mercantile. She'd finished knitting the scarves for the girls and she'd had enough yarn left to also make some red socks for Jake, but that wasn't going to be her real gift. She knew he'd have fun with the red socks, but she wanted to give him something that would show him what he was coming to mean to her.

She'd held back several of the pies she'd made and planned to give a couple of them to Wells and Higgins. The rest would be for Jake and the girls. She had jars of her rhubarb jam set aside for Annabelle and Virginia.

This was going to be a special Christmas, Elizabeth

told herself, as she packed the basket full of the cookies she'd baked last night for the children.

Miles City was busy when Jake drove the wagon down the street toward the mercantile. Annabelle was going to keep the baby for them again today. Elizabeth was looking forward to having the pageant over so she could spend more time at home with the little one.

"I don't see Spotted Fawn's pony," Jake mentioned as they pulled close to the schoolhouse. The children's horses were always tethered on the left side of the schoolhouse, out of the way of the comings and goings from the schoolhouse. There were no horses there today.

"Maybe they moved the horses somewhere because of the pageant," Elizabeth said.

Jake grunted. "They probably didn't look good enough for Mrs. Barker. She's probably got them hidden behind some bush someplace."

Elizabeth grinned. "You could be right. I hope, for her sake, that that railroad man doesn't even come. Her cousin might have been all wrong about it."

"Well, someone from the railroad is going to show up sooner or later. I guess now is as good of a time as any."

Jake helped Elizabeth unload her pies and cookies. They could hear the shrieks of the children playing behind the schoolhouse so the room was empty.

"It must be lunch," Elizabeth said as she walked over to the teacher's desk that had been pushed in a corner.

Elizabeth and Virginia had decided to put the food there so it wouldn't interfere with the performance space being used by the children. The red calico that had been left after all of the ornaments were made was lying there on the desk, ready to be spread over the food. The tree itself had been moved to the side, as well.

Elizabeth had to admit as she surveyed the empty room that a taller tree would be nice. The tree they had lacked majesty. But, Elizabeth reminded herself, it had been decorated with love and that's what the children would remember.

Jake put the last of the pies on the top of the desk. "It's a good thing you're going to cover these up. Even Higgins won't be able to keep those boys in line."

"I don't think Higgins is going to be here today. Annabelle said he was going to be helping her with something at the mercantile."

"Well, then we better be sure everything's covered before everyone gets back from lunch."

Elizabeth smiled. "Virginia keeps those boys in line almost as well as Higgins."

Jake nodded. "That's because they're all half in love with her."

Elizabeth felt her smile freeze. "I suppose all men would—"

Jake didn't even let her finish. He stepped over and gave her a hug that half lifted her off the floor.

"Not all men," he whispered when he finally put her back down.

"Oh," Elizabeth breathed. "Oh."

Elizabeth thought Jake would have kissed her if they hadn't heard the pounding of little feet on the porch of the school.

"I guess lunch is over," Jake said. He didn't move away from her, though.

"Yes, I—" Elizabeth stepped back and smoothed down the folds in her dress. "I should get ready to help with the practice—for the pageant."

Jake nodded. "And there's always more wood to chop."

The children were only starting to come back into the schoolroom when Mrs. Barker marched into the room. "Where's my ornaments?"

Elizabeth watched in fascination as the woman walked right up to the front. She should have been a drill sergeant. "I suppose you're putting them on that pathetic excuse for a tree."

Mrs. Barker lifted the Christmas tree up by its top and spun it around in front of her nose so fast a few of the pine needles fell off.

"I can assure you, the only ornaments we have are the ones the children made," Elizabeth said as she walked up to the front, as well. If someone didn't stop the woman, they wouldn't have a tree left. "Maybe you misplaced them."

Mrs. Barker humphed, but at least she put the tree down. "No one misplaces ornaments that expensive."

"Well, then, maybe Elias knows where they are," Elizabeth said as she turned around to look for the boy. The children were still coming into the room, but usually the boy was easy to find because of his red hair.

She didn't see Elias and eventually she noticed that what she did see was guilt spread across the face of every child as they came into the room.

"What's wrong?" Elizabeth asked as the reverend came inside the room with the last of the children. Elizabeth looked at him. "Where's Elias?"

"Surely, you don't think my own son—" Mrs. Barker sputtered.

"Elias didn't come to school today," the reverend said. "I thought he must be sick."

"Elias is never sick," Mrs. Barker said and then her face started to change. Fear seemed to be struggling with annoyance. "He's not off on one of those pranks of his, is he?"

Jake was looking over the children, too.

"Spotted Fawn isn't here, either," he finally said.

Dear Lord, Elizabeth breathed. *Have mercy on us.* She was hoping she'd just overlooked the girl as the others came through the door.

"Where are they?" Jake asked, facing the children.

"Did Spotted Fawn do something to my boy?" Mrs. Barker demanded. "I always said we just can't trust those people."

"Silence," Jake roared.

Mrs. Barker stopped, her mouth half-open.

"You're scaring the children," Jake said to her as he turned back to the students. "Now, who's going to tell me what's going on?"

Anna Larson, the girl who had warmed up to Spotted Fawn the most in Elizabeth's opinion, started to whimper. "Spotted Fawn hasn't done anything. She's only trying to—to help Elias."

"My son doesn't need help—"

Jake glared over at the woman until she stopped.

"Now, what are Elias and Spotted Fawn doing?" Jake turned back to the girl and asked, his voice gentle this time.

Anna gulped. "Elias said he was going to get that tree he's seen. He wanted to surprise his mother. You know, like a Christmas present. He even took the ornaments so he could have it all decorated when he brought it back to town for the pageant tonight."

"He went to get a tree for me?" Mrs. Barker looked astounded.

Anna nodded. "We weren't supposed to tell. It's a surprise."

"We understand," Elizabeth said as she stepped forward. "But what about Spotted Fawn? Where's Spotted Fawn?"

"She tried to stop him from going. She said the snows are coming. But Elias wouldn't stay—" Anna lifted her chin proudly "—so Spotted Fawn went after him to save his life like the Bible says she should—on account of him being her enemy and all."

"Well, surely, no one's saving anyone's life," Mrs. Barker said as she looked up at Jake. "There's no danger of him dying out there, is there? He'll just get the tree and come back here."

All of the irritation drained out of Jake's face and he looked at the woman with pity. "There is no tree around here, not like the one he thinks he's seen. But I'll go after them. The ground is bare so I should be able to track them with no problem. I don't expect snow until tonight at the earliest."

"I'll pack up some of the cookies," Elizabeth said as she moved toward the table they'd set up with food. "They'll be hungry."

Jake nodded.

He looked back at the children. "I assume Elias is riding that big bay he has?"

He got a dozen nods.

"Well, that's a blessing at least. That's a fine horse and should do him some good if he does run into snow," Jake said.

Elizabeth bit back her worry about Spotted Fawn's horse. She assured herself that the pony might be small, but it had been trained by the Indians. It should know just as much about snow as Elias's big bay.

Elizabeth looked down to tie the cookies in a piece of cloth and, when she looked up again, Jake was standing close. He opened his arms and she went into them as naturally as she drew her next breath.

"Don't worry," Jake whispered. "I'll get our daughter back."

"Please." Elizabeth nodded against his chest.

This time when Jake bent his head to kiss her, Elizabeth didn't care who was watching them, she kissed him back with all of the love and hope she had inside of her.

Elizabeth blinked a few times as she watched Jake walk to the door.

Jake hadn't gotten off the porch before Higgins came down the street, riding one horse and trailing another one behind him. Jake swung into the saddle of the extra horse and the two men started to ride north.

Elizabeth walked out on the porch in time to see Annabelle and Tommy come walking to the school-house. Annabelle was carrying the baby.

"Tommy told us," Annabelle said as she hurried toward Elizabeth. "Don't worry. Clarence and Jake will find them."

"I know," Elizabeth said as she turned back to go inside the schoolhouse. "They have to find them."

"I wish I could stay," Annabelle said as she took a couple of steps with Elizabeth anyway. "But I have to get back to the store. Send Tommy over to tell me when they come back."

"It shouldn't be long, should it?" Elizabeth stopped walking and looked over at her friend.

Annabelle shook her head. "Elias and Spotted Fawn have probably already turned back. But I'll be praying for them."

"Me, too," Elizabeth said.

Annabelle gave her a reassuring smile before she started walking away from the schoolhouse.

Elizabeth put a confident smile on her face before she stepped into the schoolroom. God would answer their prayers for safety. Besides, Jake hadn't thought the snowstorm would come for hours so there was really no need to worry.

Elizabeth sat in the back of the schoolroom while the angels rehearsed their songs. Mrs. Barker sat in the back, too, although she was on the Miles City side of the room and Elizabeth was sitting on the Dry Creek side.

An hour had passed when Danny came running up the stairs.

"He's here," the boy announced when the singers stopped for a breath.

"Elias?" Mrs. Barker said joyfully as she stood up.

Danny shook his head. "No, it's that railroad man. He just went into Colter's for something to drink."

"Well, we can't leave him at Colter's," Mrs. Barker said as she waved her hand at Danny. "We want the man to see the best of our community. Take him over to the mercantile."

"Me?" Danny asked in astonishment.

"You're right," Mrs. Barker said. "I'll need to go get him myself. You just run and tell Colter to bring the man outside of his establishment. Maybe I'll take him to the restaurant and buy him a nice dinner."

"It's two o'clock in the afternoon," the reverend said from the front of the room. "He's probably already had something to eat."

"Then he'll have pie." Mrs. Barker pursed her lips.

Elizabeth looked at the other woman and had pity. "He could come back here for pie. I have dried apple, pecan and berry. That way you can be here when the children come back."

Mrs. Barker nodded. "Thank you. That's very…ah… thank you."

As the woman walked out of the schoolhouse, Elizabeth thought Mrs. Barker had lost most of her starch. She didn't even leave any last-minute instructions on how they were to impress the railroad man.

Still, Elizabeth knew it was important to the woman and to the town.

Elizabeth stood up and motioned to Virginia.

They sent the children outside for an early recess and the two women set up a nice place for the railroad man to eat. They moved the doughnuts and cookies to the cabinet by the window and put a plate and fork at the teacher's desk with a folded napkin to the side.

"I could make him some coffee," the reverend said. "I have my pot in the back. It's not that green coffee, either. It's good."

"That would be nice."

"I don't suppose you could sing some for him?" Elizabeth asked Virginia. "You have such a lovely voice. That's sure to make a good impression."

By the time Mrs. Barker brought the railroad man back with her, everything was ready.

"Oh," Mrs. Barker said when she stepped in the schoolhouse and saw what they had done. Then she smiled. "Isn't this nice? Mr. Jamison, I'd like you to meet some of my—well, my friends."

Elizabeth didn't listen to the rest of the introductions. She felt pleased that Mrs. Barker had finally decided to call them friends. Spotted Fawn would be happy to know that treating one's enemies as friends did sometimes work.

Thinking of Spotted Fawn made her go to the side window of the room and look out again. The clouds were a little darker than they had been earlier. Even if it didn't snow today, darkness would come earlier than usual. Elizabeth looked out into the vastness, squinting to see as far as she could across the land here. She could see to the squat mountains north of here, but there were no signs of anyone on horseback.

Lord, she prayed. *Bring them all home safe. Please.*

Chapter Eighteen

Mr. Jamison seemed to take a long time eating his pie. Virginia kept singing and the reverend had joined the children outside to organize a spelling bee.

"This is a lovely community," Elizabeth said as she walked to the front of the schoolroom.

"Oh, yes," Mrs. Barker agreed.

Elizabeth thought the other woman sounded half-hearted. And she knew why when the woman took a peek at the watch she wore as a brooch.

"My, it's getting cooler outside," Mrs. Barker said as she stood up from the bench where she was sitting and began to wander the schoolroom as Elizabeth was doing. "I hope that doesn't mean the snow will come earlier than we expected."

"Don't worry about the snow," Mr. Jamison said as he pushed back his empty plate. "Now, that's some of the finest pie I've ever had in my life."

Elizabeth nodded. "Thank you. So you don't think the snow's coming soon?"

"Oh, I expect the snow will come, I just don't think there'll be much of it." Mr. Jamison brushed at his lips with the napkin. "I stopped at the fort before I came over here and they were sending several patrols out. I don't think they'd be doing that if a blizzard was expected."

"No, no, I suppose not," Elizabeth said with a frown. She knew the soldiers didn't go out on patrol in winter unless it was important. "You don't happen to know—"

Just then Colter walked into the schoolhouse. He was wearing a gun belt and carrying a rifle. "A soldier just came to my place and said the patrols are heading north of here."

Elizabeth felt her breath stop. "North of here? That's the way Jake and Higgins went. What's north of here?"

Colter had a trapped look on his face. "Now, there's no need to worry. I just wanted to let Virginia know I was—"

"What's—north—of—here?" Elizabeth barely got the words out.

Colter didn't answer.

But Mr. Jamison did. "I expect it's those renegades the patrols are out looking for."

"Oh, dear," Mrs. Barker said as she sank down to the nearest bench. "My Elias is out there with those savages?"

"Not to mention Spotted Fawn, Jake and Higgins," Elizabeth added.

"Of course," Mrs. Barker mumbled.

"I'm hoping to catch up with Jake and Higgins," Colter said. "They can't have gone far yet."

"You can't—" Virginia started to say.

But Colter had already left the schoolroom.

There was silence for a minute.

"I don't know if the railroad is interested in places that have this much trouble with the savages still," Mr. Jamison finally said as he stood up.

"Oh, who cares," Mrs. Barker wailed. "They might have my baby."

"Of course," Mr. Jamison said. "Perhaps I should go back to my hotel and wait for the performance this evening. I assume it's still going to be held?"

"We don't know," Elizabeth managed to say as she took a step toward Virginia and then one toward Mrs. Barker, both of whom were in tears.

"Ah, well—yes, of course." Mr. Jamison cleared his throat and then walked down the aisle and out of the schoolroom.

The three women met in the middle of the room and hugged each other until Mrs. Barker's hat fell off and Virginia's eyes grew red from crying. Elizabeth was the first to pull away.

"We have things to do while we wait," Elizabeth said. "We need to…ah…"

Surely, there were things they needed to do, Elizabeth thought. "We could bring in some wood so it'll be plenty warm when they get back."

"And I could go get some of that tonic I use to ward off a cough," Mrs. Barker said.

"First, we need to pray," Virginia said and the three women came together again. They just stood there in silence, each pleading with God.

When they parted, Elizabeth felt a need to go over to the mercantile and hold the baby. Annabelle had been tending the little one while Elizabeth was helping with the pageant, but no one was going to be rehearsing this afternoon.

Annabelle was stepping out of the mercantile when Elizabeth was walking down the street toward the building. The other woman had the baby in her arms.

"Oh, I just heard," Annabelle said when she looked up and saw Elizabeth. "I was coming over to talk to you."

Annabelle held out the baby and Elizabeth took the little one and snuggled her to her chest.

"We can talk inside as well as anywhere," Annabelle said as she turned around and opened the door. "Business has been slow today anyway."

"Thank you," Elizabeth said as she followed the other woman inside.

Annabelle led Elizabeth back to her small parlor. "Here, make yourself comfortable. I'll heat some water for tea."

"That would be nice."

Elizabeth let the peace of Annabelle's parlor wash over her as she held the baby.

It was all happening again. And she was completely helpless. She was just starting to love this new family and God was taking it away from her.

"I don't know how you did it," Elizabeth said as Annabelle brought her a cup of tea. "How did you recover from two husbands dying?"

Annabelle sat down with her own cup of tea. "Well,

it wasn't easy. It was worse with Tommy's father than with my last husband. I thought I'd never get over him."

"You must have loved him more."

Annabelle shook her head. "No, I think I loved him less. It was the guilt that made it so hard with him. It would just grind at me. I felt like if I grieved deeper it would make up for not loving him so much when he was alive."

"I know. It's the betrayal," Elizabeth said. "Me being alive and him being dead. I know I loved Rose more than Matthew, but I think I'm going to be able to let her go. But Matthew…I just…"

"Believe me, I know."

"It seems wrong to be falling in love with Jake," Elizabeth finally said. "What does that say about Matthew?"

"Listen to me Elizabeth O'Brian Hargrove," Annabelle said. "You did your best by your Matthew. That's all you could do. Leave the rest in God's hands. You can't live in the past. Not when God's giving you a new family to love."

"Yes, but—" Elizabeth started and then blinked. Tears were starting in her eyes and she blinked again. "I'm sorry, I don't—" tears started streaming down Elizabeth's cheeks "—cry."

Annabelle stood up and came over to pat Elizabeth on the shoulder. "Of course, you cry. We all do."

"It's just that…I—I never told Jake…and now he's out there. And Spotted Fawn…I never told her. And…"

"You'll tell them," Annabelle said firmly. "They're coming back and you'll tell them how you feel. My Clarence will see that they come back. And, just in case he has a bit of trouble, we're going to sit right here and pray."

Elizabeth wiped her eyes and bowed her head.

"Lord, protect those we love," Annabelle prayed. "We know they're in Your hands. Amen."

Elizabeth looked up. "Thank you."

The bell rang out in the store and Annabelle walked to the door of her parlor. "You just sit there now and relax. I'll let you know if anyone hears something."

Elizabeth nodded. She lifted the baby up to her shoulder and rubbed the little one's back.

"God's going to bring your uncle home," she whispered to the infant. "And your big sister, too."

Elizabeth hoped she was right. She didn't care what Annabelle said. She didn't think her second loss would be easier than her first. She had barely made it through losing Matthew; she couldn't lose Jake, too. Especially not like this, with him not even knowing that she cared about him.

All of the anger she'd felt toward God didn't mean much to her right now, not when she needed Him so much.

Elizabeth sat and held the baby until she saw the first snowflake fall outside the window in Annabelle's parlor.

"Oh, dear." Elizabeth stood up. She needed to go back to the schoolhouse and make sure someone was keeping the fire up.

"I'm closing here in a half hour," Annabelle said as Elizabeth told her she was going. "I'll be over there then."

Elizabeth nodded.

"Everyone will probably be back by then anyway," Annabelle said. "The way this whole town is praying, they've just got to be back soon."

Elizabeth had snow on her and the baby when she got back to the schoolhouse. The room was nice and warm when she stepped inside. Everyone looked behind them when Elizabeth opened the door.

"It's just me," Elizabeth said as she started to brush the snow off as best she could with one hand.

The reverend had gathered the children to the front of the room and it looked as though he was reading them a story from the Bible. Virginia was sitting off to the side listening, as well.

"I didn't know it was snowing that much," Virginia said as she walked back to Elizabeth. "Colter didn't even take a coat."

"He probably has a blanket in the bedroll behind his saddle," Elizabeth said.

"I know, but—" Virginia said and then sighed. "I worry. He's my boss, you know."

Elizabeth smiled. "I know."

"Sometimes, I think…" Virginia started. "But it's impossible. Not with him believing the way he does and me—"

Elizabeth nodded. "I know."

The two women sat together and waited. Finally, Mrs. Barker came back to the schoolhouse, too.

"I was writing a letter to Elias's father," she said as she sat down with Virginia and Elizabeth. "Then I got so mad that he isn't here that I just tore it up. A boy needs his father."

"I know you miss them both," Elizabeth said.

"I noticed Elias took an old coat of his father's this morning. I should have seen that earlier. My husband always wore that coat when he went out riding with Elias at this time of year."

"At least he'll be warm," Elizabeth said. All of a sudden she wished fiercely that she'd let Spotted Fawn keep wearing those leggings of hers. They'd keep her warm in the snow better than those flimsy pantalettes and stockings that she was wearing now.

"I'm sure your girl will be fine, too," Mrs. Barker said as she put her hand on Elizabeth's arm.

"Thank you."

Virginia was the one who suggested that everyone sing some hymns. The children had been singing Christmas carols all week so they settled into the familiar sounds of their favorite hymns easily.

"Some of these children have a real love for music," Virginia said after one song. She'd come back to sit with the women while the children each had an apple fried doughnut from the basket Elizabeth had brought in that morning.

"It's too bad you can't teach them," Elizabeth said.

Virginia nodded. "Maybe someday."

"Don't wait too long," Elizabeth said. "Sometimes—"

"I know," Virginia said as she stood up. "Sometimes we wait until it's too late."

Elizabeth pulled the baby close to her again.

Chapter Nineteen

Tommy saw the horses first. Dusk was just starting to make itself known and the boy had been standing by the schoolhouse window, searching through the falling snowflakes, trying to see something before it got too dark.

"They're coming! They're coming!"

Elizabeth put the baby back in the small crib she'd fashioned out of two benches and rushed to the window to look out. She could barely see the figures in the distance.

"There are three horses," Tommy announced. He paused a minute. "I wonder what happened to…" His voice trailed off.

Oh, dear, Elizabeth thought, squinting to see better in the snow. There should be five horses. The three men and the two children. "I'm sure there's some explanation."

Unfortunately, Elizabeth could not think of an explanation that was any good.

It was silent in the schoolroom, but Elizabeth could hear the quiet sobbing of Mrs. Barker.

"They didn't find them," the other woman finally said. "My baby's gone and it's all my fault. If I hadn't made such a fuss about that Christmas tree, he would have never gone out there and—"

Elizabeth walked over to the woman. "Hush now, you had no idea at the time what would happen. We can't control everything that happens in life."

Elizabeth opened her arms and the other woman walked right into them.

"We're not God," Elizabeth finally murmured as she patted Mrs. Barker on the back. Elizabeth knew how the other woman felt; guilty for not being able to foresee what would happen to the ones she loved.

God forgive me for trying to be You, Elizabeth prayed silently as she felt her old resentments melt away.

"They're coming fast," Tommy yelled.

Both women rushed back to the window. Sure enough, Elizabeth saw, the horses were coming in at a slow gallop.

"Oh, dear, what now?" Elizabeth said as she turned to hurry out onto the porch.

The three horses came stomping up to the porch, tossing their heads and prancing a little. A cheer rose up from the children waiting on the porch. Everyone was home.

Spotted Fawn was sharing a horse with Jake and Elias was riding behind Higgins's saddle. Colter rode alone, but he wore a grin as big as the other two men did.

"Thank God," Annabelle said when the cheering died down.

"We thought you might worry once you could see us," Jake said. "So we hurried up here."

Elizabeth just looked up at her husband. He wasn't wearing his hat and his hair was blown this way and that. The cold had made his face pale. And yet he was the most handsome man she'd ever seen. He had her heart.

"Spotted Fawn saved my life," Elias leaned around Higgins and announced from the back of the horse. "Those Indians were going to scalp me and Spotted Fawn said they had to take her hair first."

"Oh, dear Lord," Mrs. Barker gasped.

Elizabeth echoed the sentiment but she was so speechless not even a gasp escaped.

"Of course, they didn't want hers on account of who she is." Elias kept going. "She can talk to them and everything."

"Of course she can talk to them." Mrs. Barker finally got her breath back. "She's one of them."

There was a moment's silence.

"Not that," Mrs. Barker added with a reluctant little smile. "Not that she's not one of us, too, now."

"She's just got a brown skin is all," Anna said decisively from where she was standing along with the other children. "Like Elias has got that red hair of his and I have my blue eyes. It's all just different colors, but the same underneath."

"That's why they wanted my scalp," Elias said, still excited over his adventure. "That Indians said they'd never seen such red hair. It'd make a good—whatever they use them for."

Elizabeth stepped off the porch and walked over to Jake's horse. She put up her arms and Jake lifted Spotted Fawn off the horse and into them. Elizabeth gently set Spotted Fawn on the ground so she could hug the girl properly.

"I love you," Elizabeth whispered into Spotted Fawn's ear. The girl stood a little stiffly in Elizabeth's arms, but she still had a small smile on her face the whole time she was being hugged.

"What happened to the other horses?" Tommy asked as he looked around.

"We traded for them," Elias explained as he slid off Higgins's horse. "At first, Spotted Fawn offered our horses for my scalp and they were thinking about it, trying to decide if it was a good deal or not on account of my hair being so special. And then Spotted Fawn opened the saddlebag on my horse and brought out those ornaments—"

"My Christmas ornaments!" Mrs. Barker was aghast. "Don't tell me you broke those ornaments. They came from Germany."

"We didn't break them. Spotted Fawn traded them for my scalp."

"Well, what would those Indians possibly want with the things. They don't even celebrate Christmas," Mrs. Barker snapped. "They're handblown glass berries and nuts and apples and—my word, don't tell me they tried to eat the things."

Elias shook his head. "Spotted Fawn put each of the ornaments on some yarn and the Indians are wearing them around their necks. One of them even had a big grizzly paw around his neck and he took it off to wear a pear. I thought maybe he'd give me the grizzly paw, but he didn't. Anyway, they like the ornaments. But they said they weren't enough so they also got the promise of more Christmas presents."

"What presents?" Mrs. Barker looked around.

"We're supposed to go leave them presents of food in the ravine by the schoolhouse tomorrow and they'll leave us our horses back."

Mrs. Barker looked up at the men. "I thought you were supposed to get everything back."

"Spotted Fawn had already made the trade when we got there," Jake said. "It wouldn't be honorable to back down then."

"Well, I've never heard of such a thing," Mrs. Barker said.

Over the next few hours, that phrase was repeated often. Elizabeth suspected it was partially because of Elias. The tale of his nearly being scalped got bigger each time he told the story. The band of renegades grew from eight to nearly eighty. The knife grew to the size of a sword. The grizzly paw became a whole leg of the animal. And Spotted Fawn grew from being his rescuer to the one he bravely rescued.

Spotted Fawn didn't seem to mind. She was busy getting ready to be an angel for the pageant. Since all of the children were still at the schoolhouse and there had been no way to let most of the parents know about the excitement of the afternoon, it was decided they should just go ahead with the pageant.

"You're quite the angel," Elizabeth said as she straightened Spotted Fawn's wings for the tenth time. "I just don't want you to go riding out like that again."

Spotted Fawn nodded. "I don't think Elias will go."

"Yes, well, you shouldn't go with anyone, unless it's your uncle, of course. Or some other adult that your uncle and I approve of."

Spotted Fawn nodded. "Like Mr. Higgins."

"Yes, it's safe to ride to school with Mr. Higgins."

Elizabeth squared the shoulders on Spotted Fawn's white union suit and decided her daughter did look a little like an angel.

The pageant eventually started with the stars gliding onto the stage area at the front of the room. A dozen coal oil lamps were sitting on shelves and they made the whole inside of the schoolhouse look golden. The stars painted on the front wall even glistened a little. Mrs. Barker had moved the small tree from where it stood at the side of the room to the middle of the stage area, declaring it was a perfect tree for a pageant. The red calico ornaments on the tree stood out brightly since someone had hung a lamp on the ceiling over the tree.

The parents were sitting on the school benches, none of them paying attention to which side of the line they were on. The railroad man was sitting in the front row and he wasn't frowning, so Elizabeth took that as a good sign. She and Jake were in the back. Jake had brought his shoulder sling so the baby could sleep if she wanted. Elizabeth liked being able to see everyone in her family, even Spotted Fawn, who was standing so close to her friend, Anna, that their wings were probably tangled by now.

The reverend, looking dignified and solemn, walked out onstage with the stars.

"'In the time of King Herod,'" the reverend started to read from his Bible for the pageant, "wise men came from the East asking 'Where is the child who has been born king of the Jews? For we observed his star at its rising, and have come—'"

The stars were rising up and dancing while the angels began to sing.

The whole pageant was over in forty minutes. The stars finished their dancing, the shepherds heard the angels, and they all sang together of the holy night long ago. The telling of the story didn't seem as if it took much time, but Elizabeth knew the families in this community would never be the same.

Part of that was because, before the pageant, everyone had heard the story of how Spotted Fawn had gone to the rescue of Elias Barker, the boy whose mother had tried to make her an outcast. Everyone knew there would be no more talk about heathens in their midst or lines down the floor of the church.

"It's a new start for us all," Elizabeth said to Jake. The final child had just walked off the stage area and people were lining up for the food table. She and Jake were content to sit on the bench in the back of the room.

Jake nodded as he reached over and took her hand that lay on her lap.

"You're a blessing to me and the girls, Elizabeth O'Brian Hargrove."

"You're all right with me being both O'Brian and Hargrove?" Elizabeth looked up him in surprise.

"I figure if Spotted Fawn can make her peace with Elias, I can stop being jealous of a dead man."

"Oh, you have nothing to be jealous about," Elizabeth said. "You're—"

"Yes?" Jake leaned his head closer.

Elizabeth blushed. She looked around to be sure no one was listening. Even then she whispered. "You're magnificent."

Jake started to grin. "I hope that look in your eyes means you're thinking of staying with us past the spring?"

Elizabeth nodded. "It's just—"

Jake's grin started to fade. "Whatever it is, we'll work it out."

"It's not a problem," Elizabeth said. "I'd just like to have a real wedding before—you know—so we can say the words and mean them."

Jake's grin spread as his eyes deepened. "Elizabeth, will you marry me?"

Elizabeth nodded. "It would be my pleasure."

"In that case, I'm going to kiss my fiancée," Jake said as he proceeded to do just that.

Elizabeth thought she heard clapping in the distance, but that didn't make any sense. The pageant was already over. And, since it was, there seemed little harm in having another kiss. Or two.

Epilogue

Everyone gathered for the wedding on the first Sunday afternoon in May. Elizabeth had wanted to wait for a day that would be warm enough for them to have the ceremony on the banks of Dry Creek. Besides, it gave Jake time to put up the headstone he'd promised and for her to finish her mourning.

"You're a beautiful bride," Virginia said.

Elizabeth smiled over at her friend as they waited by a cottonwood tree. Virginia was her maid of honor. "Thank you. I can't believe the day is really here."

The guests were all being seated on the log benches Jake and Higgins had borrowed from the schoolhouse. Dozens of families had come from Miles City as well as some of the soldiers from the fort.

The railroad man had even ridden over. He was making his second inspection of Miles City and had already told everyone things were promising. He said he'd been impressed with the children in the town, particularly Spotted Fawn.

Elizabeth had been proud when she heard the man talk of Spotted Fawn's bravery. She looked over to where the girls were sitting now with Annabelle and Higgins.

"I can't get used to calling the baby Mary," Elizabeth whispered. Spotted Fawn had decided her sister should be named in honor of Christmas. "I always just think of her as my baby."

Virginia followed her gaze. "She'll always be your baby, no matter what her name is."

Elizabeth nodded. "I know."

They were silent for a few minutes and then Elizabeth smoothed down the folds of her moss-green velvet dress.

"Jake always did want me to have a dress this color," Elizabeth finally said. "I think he was half-afraid I was going to wear that mourning dress if he didn't buy me something new."

"Maybe you should pass the mourning dress along to me now," Virginia said with a twist to her lips.

"Oh, don't say that." Elizabeth put her hand on her friend's arm. "Colter will come back."

Virginia shrugged. "I'm not even sure I want him to—"

Colter had left town in January, saying he had business he needed to attend to before he went forward with his life. He'd left the saloon and Danny with Virginia as well as enough money to see them settled while she turned the saloon into a studio for her piano lessons.

Just then the reverend cleared his throat. The guests were seated and Jake was waiting at the front of the aisle formed by the two rows of benches.

"We'll talk later," Elizabeth said as the two women walked forward.

"No, we won't," Virginia said. "This is your wedding day and there's a man watching you now who looks like he's the happiest man alive."

"He does, doesn't he?" Elizabeth said as Virginia walked down the aisle ahead of her.

Jake was wearing a suit. Not a suit of buckskin. Not even a flannel shirt and wool pants. No, it was a suit that would do justice to a banker. He thought his mother would be proud, even of the red socks he wore on his feet.

Elizabeth almost floated down the aisle to him. She was beaming and he couldn't take his eyes off her. She was a vision in that green dress of hers, just as he'd known she would be. His Elizabeth was beautiful. She wore her old wedding ring around her neck on the gold chain he'd given her for Christmas; he had her new ring in his pocket.

When Elizabeth reached his side, she put her hand on his arm.

Jake had insisted on the longest ceremony possible this time. He wanted to promise everything to his wife. That he'd protect her. Comfort her. Provide for her. Love her.

He paused on that one. He especially wanted to promise to love her.

Elizabeth looked up at Jake as she repeated her vows. She almost had to shade her eyes, the sun was so bright behind him. She smiled; he looked all golden around the edges.

"You may now kiss the bride," Reverend Olson said

with such satisfaction in his voice that some of the guests chuckled quietly.

"Finally," the reverend added with heartfelt enthusiasm.

Elizabeth didn't care if the whole countryside erupted in joyful laughter. It was no secret that she and Jake had walked a long path to arrive at this place. She reached up and touched his cheek as he bent his head toward her. The kiss was all she'd ever dreamed it could be.

Dear Reader,

I don't know if you have ever felt like Elizabeth O'Brian, but I suspect we all have. We sit in the ashes of our dreams and wonder why God has abandoned us. I hope Elizabeth's story gives you comfort the next time it happens to you.

While writing this book, I was struck anew by the fact that our lives take many twists and turns, some of them expected and some of them not. I deliberately picked a time in Montana history when there were a lot of changes—the Indians were leaving, or, more accurately, being forced onto reservations; the railroad was coming, some towns were rising up and others were falling flat.

All too often, it's when there is great change that we hang on most tightly to our old dreams. This has been true throughout history. We like to be in control of our future, whether or not God wants it that way.

I hope you have enjoyed reading about Elizabeth's struggle with change. If you have not also read some of my contemporary Dry Creek series, please do. You'll find that the community that was born in this historical book is alive and kicking in the contemporary series.

I love to hear from my readers. If you get a chance, go to my Web site at www.JanetTronstad.com and you can send me an e-mail. If you don't have e-mail access, you can always drop me a note in care of the editors at Steeple Hills Books, 233 Brookway, Suite 1001, New York, NY 10279.

God's blessings on you!

Janet Tronstad

QUESTIONS FOR DISCUSSION

1. Elizabeth O'Brian was mad at God because of the death of her husband and baby. Do you think this is a normal part of grief? Have you ever been that mad at God?

2. Sometimes anger at God hangs on for a long time. What are some ways to deal with this when it happens to us?

3. Jake Hargrove was willing to raise his nieces, because there seemed to be no other option for them. He didn't know how he would do it, though. Can you think of things in your life that God has called you to do and you wonder how you will manage? What happened in those situations?

4. Elizabeth had a hard time letting go of her old life. What were some of the reasons for this?

5. Elizabeth was warned about marrying Jake because the store clerk thought he was a wolfer. What is a wolfer? Why were they so despised by people in the West?

6. The townspeople, under the leadership of Mrs. Barker, refused to welcome Jake and his new family into the church. Why? Did you have some sympathy for the townspeople? Why or why not?

7. Do similar things happen in your church today? What groups have you struggled to welcome?

8. Spotted Fawn was teased at school. Have you or a child you know been teased at school? What did you do about it? What can a child do? What can parents do when this happens to their children?

9. Spotted Fawn struggled to love her enemies at school. Have you ever had to love someone who was not kind to you? What did you do?

10. Jake had to be patient as he came to love Elizabeth, because she was not ready to love him. From Elizabeth's viewpoint, what things stood in the way of loving Jake? Have you ever needed someone to be patient with you before you loved them—a parent, husband, God?